It's a hell of a thing, killing a man.
You take away all he's got and all he's ever gonna have.

—William Munny, *Unforgiven*

The devil promised that all his people should live bravely,
that all persons should be equal,
that there should be no day of resurrection or of judgment,
and neither punishment nor shame for sin.

—The confession of William Barker Sr.
at the Salem witch trials

DEVIL'S CALL

J. DANIELLE DORN

Published by Inkshares, Inc., Oakland, California
www.inkshares.com

Edited by Adam Gomolin, Philip Sciranka, and Staton Rabin
Cover design by David Drummond
Interior design by Kevin G. Summers

ISBN: 9781942645603
e-ISBN: 9781942645610
Library of Congress Control Number: 2017940695

First edition

Printed in the United States of America

I

BEFORE I LEAVE YOU in this world, my dear, I aim to record what came to pass when your momma rode from the Nebraska Territory to Louisiana to the frozen Badlands to bring to justice the monster who murdered your father.

I know you will have more questions than I will be able to answer in these pages. Some of those questions your Nana Cat will answer, as she answered mine when I wondered about the world and my place in it. If our path is freer and easier than it has been thus far, you will grow up in a family of witches proud and strong, and one day you will understand why you did so without a mother or a father. Why there was no other way this story was going to end.

It was not my intention for you to come into this world not knowing your father, and I sure as hell did not intend for you to not know your mother, but what I am about to tell you is an injustice the likes of which the world has been tolerating for so long as men have walked in it.

Bringing you into that kind of world is nothing your father and I envisioned when we set out to start a family. We did the best we could with what we had, which was not much. I liked to think it was enough.

When I dream of you grown, I dream you have your father Matthew's eyes, bright and blue and kind, some mischief in them but no malice. When I dream of you, I dream of him. I cannot help it. His ghost, I suspect, will follow you a long time.

Your father was a tall man, and handsome, at least to my eyes. He spoke little, and he spoke even less of his life before the war. He joined the United States Army in the fall of 1843 at the age of seventeen, and three years later when the call came for men to fight in Mexico, he answered. He was a doctor, and a good one, and though he did not fear violence, acting on it was not in his nature. He went to Mexico to patch up those who did fight. From hearing him speak of his time there, the oath he swore as a doctor and the oath he swore as a soldier were at odds with each other.

Folks in town respected your father for his part in the war almost as much as they respected him for his work as a doctor, but I know they feared I had him under a spell, that he was with me not because of love but because he had no choice. You will hear folks call love by many different names, but love and infatuation are not the same, and even the world's most powerful witch cannot force a man to love her.

I hear a lot of things other folks don't. Folks mistake me for Indian if they do not mistake me for Mexican, and they cease minding their tongues around those they think to be beneath them anyway. I have light eyes same as your father did, which I suppose frightens them more than accounts of my witchcraft do. Dark eyes in a face like mine would make sense to them, but light eyes do not.

What your father saw and did during the war trailed after him even after he took off his spurs. He likened it to a dog he had fed once keeping at his heel in the hopes he would drop another scrap. Having moments of violence in his past, he thought, meant he would always be a man of violence. But he never raised a hand to another person in his life. Never touched a weapon after he hung his up for the last time. But the war changed him.

Changed or not, I loved him. None of this would have happened if I did not love him.

2

YOU COME FROM a long line of women gifted in a way that scares most folks.

According to the stories your gran told me when I was young, our family's roots grew deep in Scottish soil. Our ancestors lived in a small town known as Marc Innis, or Horse Meadow, which was once an island in the midst of a lake a long time past.

The women in this family have always run a public house, healing and helping in our blood, but so too have we always lived in fear of fire. Five times the Church of Scotland roved through the Lowlands, seeking out the accursed, pricking them with devices that would prove a woman was caught in the devil's snare. Five times the Church of Scotland strung up the women in our family, and five times they burned them alive.

One of the earliest stories I remember concerns the fate of my great-great-great-grandmother Eimhir, who practiced necromancy when she could not accept the death of her beloved. She was one of the last to burn before our line departed the land that had sustained us for so long.

The women in this family are stubborn, but they are not stupid. Those who were able gathered up what little they needed to survive at sea and left the country in the 1600s. They were indentured servants in the beginning, working for the English in the New World.

Perhaps your gran will give you a greater account of how the roadhouse came to rest in their hands, but the way I heard it, one of her aunts married the fellow who owned the place, and the fellow did not die so much as he crawled inside a whiskey bottle and curled up at the bottom of it. It was just as well. If he had died before he gave her a son, your great-great-aunt would have had no recourse, legal or otherwise, for hanging on to the place.

The men in this family do not have the gift the women have. As near as I can tell, it has more to do with blood than with the body. Always in our histories, men have been responsible for keeping us rooted in the world. If not for them coming into the wilds aiming to tame it, we would have stayed wild ourselves, nettles in our hair and dirt for lip color. Such is the way of wild things.

Ours is not a religion. It is a way of life, and it is an abomination to those who do not understand it. The roadhouse is a sanctuary for us. I grew wild with your aunts and cousins in the nursery while men gambled and drank and smoked beneath our twiglet dolls and pretend altars.

Before I knew what it was to be a witch, I knew what it was to be different.

My wildness came from not knowing who my father was. You will have stories of your momma and your daddy both. I had only my imagination. From my imagination I drew pictures of highwaymen and wayward sons and rebellious heirs. Only in the mirror could I see traces of who he might have been. My hair was thick and black while my cousins had fine curls, red in the winter months and corn silk in the summer. While their eyes were big and green, their skin fair and freckled, my eyes were not so round and my skin would brown like bread by summer's end. It freckled, sure, but I did not have to protect my skin the way my cousins had to protect theirs.

My earliest memory is of the nursery we shared. Sunlight from one window and the smell of the herbs from the back garden from the other. The rug beneath us as old as the roadhouse itself, older. If we aligned our tiny fingers with the piles, all of us in a circle, we could convince each other we heard the voices of the women who wove it, our ancestors, our blood. Girlhood is a magick all its own, and our girlhood was a shared one.

My mother dreaded my first day of school. In the week leading up to it, she stopped smiling altogether, started snapping her fingers to get our attention, slapping our wrists when we slipped up. Pulling a glass across the breakfast table with our Will instead of asking if someone would please pass the milk, or sharing our thoughts using mental projection instead of our words, shattering the silence with causeless giggling—these things would draw attention to us in a room full of strangers. We were young, and we were careless. Our wrists were red from all the disciplining by the time the aunts lined us up in the nursery to sit between their knees as they combed and braided our hair.

My mother had to comb mine with a particular fierceness, as it preferred to fall in waves. And though she smoothed the waves with a wetted palm, the baby hairs along the edge of my scalp would not lie flat. She stood me up when the braiding was done and held me still and called me her smart, brave girl before leaving the room, leaving my cousin Eva holding up our plaits side by side as if she had never noticed their contrasting color before.

"Look how dark your hair is, Lily," she said to me. None of the younger girls could pronounce my name, Li Lian, given to honor my faceless father.

Some lessons I could learn from watching the other girls. I learned to braid a lilac flower into my hair to bring wisdom during lessons or to sprinkle playing cards with nutmeg to bring the dealer good fortune. Physical objects can serve as a focus for your magick, and they can also make less obvious the fact that you are using your Will to change the world around you.

Other lessons I had to learn myself. There are lessons you will have to learn for yourself. Some I hope like hell you will learn from what I have recorded here, though I am beginning to believe so far as hope is concerned, mine has run its course.

Every day on the way to school, we passed by the riverfront, where the men would unload the big boats, and horses would pull crates to meet up with the railroad. From time to time after school, we would walk along the railroad to collect coins and horseshoes and other metal objects abandoned along the tracks.

During my fourth year, when I was near the age of nine or so, I began to believe trouble and I were destined to spend our lives together. The lesson of the day concerned the advent of the steam engine and its implications, and the younger children were excused to the yard to practice their lessons or play, and I remember clear as yesterday a little blond boy named Daniel Chesterfield sticking his hand into the air and calling out without waiting for the teacher to give him permission.

Our schoolmistress was a thin woman with a long, sad face. I remember overhearing a remark that she was not much older than my cousin Agnes, Eva's eldest sister, and though she was a maiden, she had the weary disposition of a crone. She did not want to ask Danny to repeat himself, this I could hear in her bones, but she did anyway.

"The men who work on the steamboats," Danny said. "They all look like Lilian."

"No, they don't!" I said, because the men who worked on the steamboats were covered in dirt and coal dust and sweat, and though I would not hesitate to dig in the dirt with my bare hands, I did not spend my days in that state.

"Yes, they do," he said, and then he put a thumb to the corner of either eye and pulled back the skin.

I threw my chalkboard at him then, which earned both of us time in opposite corners of the schoolhouse while the others completed their lesson and went outside to play. Danny would go on to enlist his friends in chasing me and my friends around the yard, pushing us down and spitting on us, pulling our hair and dropping insects down the backs of our dresses. When I told my mother of Danny's reign of terror, she said, "You would do best to ignore that young man. He will get what is coming to him."

Waiting was not in my nature. If you are anything like your father, you will find yourself quick to make friends. If you are more like your mother, you will find it easier to lose them.

About the worst thing I ever did in my early life was curse that boy. Your gran was not pleased to hear from the schoolmistress that I had cut free a lock of Danny's hair with a pair of sewing scissors I had hidden away in my skirts that morning, and when she asked me what I had done with the hair, I did not want to tell her I had mixed it with cow dung and dirt and deposited it in the gutter for the water to carry away. I had, so I denied having been anywhere near the boy. When we learned he had taken to bed with dysentery, I told your gran he must have drunk out of the river like he was not supposed to.

Maybe she could have proven I was the one who made him ill, and shown me the proof. She did not. Nor did she lecture or punish me.

If I were born in Salem times and done to Danny what I done, folks would have dragged me in front of the judge and hanged me that afternoon. Eight is plenty old enough to die when the law thinks what you done is rotten enough. Luck and I have always had an understanding, but I know now the fear your gran felt for me after what I did in the schoolyard. Killing Danny on accident would have made this a different story, and a shorter one.

The same day Danny failed to appear for lessons, I too found myself beset by stomach ailments. I shall spare you the details, but I spent more time in the outhouse than I did at my desk, and when I returned home that afternoon ashen and sweat-soaked, your gran shook her head and asked me, "Was it worth it?"

Our powers come with a price. All power, I suppose, comes with a price. Your father would have had a scientific explanation for this property, cited a Newtonian law to explain nature's love of balance. We have a simpler explanation for it—the law of three. What energy one sends out, whether it be fair or foul, returns threefold. While I am certain I suffered far greater pains than did Danny, he did not go home to a family of healers, and when we returned to school, the wind had gone out of his sails. He no longer ran about the yard as he once did.

Danny did not recognize what I had done as witchcraft, and he did not report it as such. But when in the yard in front of his friends he accused me of making him sick, I told him it was me who turned his guts to water and to leave my friends alone or it would be worse the next time.

He never came near any of us girls again, but neither did anyone else.

I hope you grow up to be a wild one, that you learn to spit and curse and shoot a gun. This country is not kind to soft women. Maybe back east it is. Back east I hear they drape their women in lace and gild their homes and change their clothing a half a dozen times a day. St. Louis is considerably more civilized than the frontier, where your home would have been, where we do not have such things. I wish I could say the openness of the plains and the danger waiting on those who go out into it un-prepared would be enough to make men kinder to one another, but I do not believe it to be in a man's nature to be kind. Hard times make for hard men.

Be wild, but be wise, darling.

I hope you will recognize the darkness in this story, that you will see your momma not as brave and bold but as stubborn and angry. I hope you will take after your father in temperament. Be kind and patient. Ask questions and know when to accept what is in front of you.

Even after all this time, I miss him. I should have been more careful.

When you are old enough, I hope you find a good man, brave and kind. I hope you take more care than I have.

You are the only good and pure thing to come out of all of this.

3

OF ALL THE STORIES your gran never told me, the one I wished for hardest was that of how she and your grandfather met. To this day I do not know it, but I know I will not allow you to grow up guessing at who your father might be.

When I was a girl of about thirteen, I ran away from St. Louis, not on account of any wrong my kin had done but rather my own wandering feet. I thought my destiny lay down the river where the steamboats and their passengers disappeared. I grew tired of looking into the faces of men whose names I did not know, who carried on with their work without knowing I was looking at them so. I grew tired of wondering if my father was among them, and knowing he and I would never recognize each other even if we did pass each other by in the street. So one day I gathered the money I had earned cleaning the bar at the roadhouse and I stole away on the first ship I met headed south.

Even now, I cannot tell you what I expected to find there. Texas is a long ways from Missouri, and in those days it was much as I was—seeking independence yet headed towards statehood. What happened on that journey is a story you can find in my own diary, when you are old enough to feel an itch in your soles yourself, but I will tell you now I was run away for a good four months before forces greater than I brought me home again.

My carriage and my willingness to make eye contact gave strangers the impression I was older than my age, and though it was not my intention to put down roots out there on the borderlands, I found myself inclined to stay awhile when I saw men of all shades walking the streets. On the way south I had passed a group of Waco Indian travelers, with whom I traded without incident. Once there, a half-Mexican man offered me a job in his cantina. All I had to do was ask for it. The rules were a little looser in Texas, and I felt less alien when I was among others to whom the sun was kind.

So it came to pass that at the age of fourteen I was working as a barmaid in a cantina on the north side of the Brazos River, my skin dark brown and my hair shimmering red from the sun bleaching it. On weekends, I filled mugs and poured whiskey, but during the week, on slow nights, the vaqueros and gamblers would invite me over to play a hand or two. At first they meant it as a joke, but as time passed I proved myself capable of holding my own against men with scarred faces and gold-capped teeth. The nutmeg I sprinkled on the deck when it was my turn to deal appeared like dirt in the dusty light.

Like I did most of my girlhood lessons, I learned to play cards from watching my older cousins and the roadhouse patrons. Liquor has a way of making men act in a way they would never in their right mind. It eats away at the part of them capable of concerning itself with civility. Monsters are not always real, my dear, save the ones that started out as men.

I am not sure if the drunk who called me a witch the day I met your father started out mean and grew meaner with time. He may well have come out of the womb the way he came into the cantina. Some folks just have meanness in their bones.

The day was slow and sultry. With the cantina empty as it was, I had taken up a place at the brag table. We were having ourselves a pleasant game with low stakes and more laughter than luck when a soldier with the United States Army swatted open the swinging doors and stepped inside. His belt was heavy with weaponry and his spurs chimed with the cadence of his pace. The owner's son, Chimalli, was tending bar that day, and though none of us were paying any mind, we all heard the stranger say to the young man, "*Oye*, varlet! Whiskey, *rápido*."

As I had my back to the door, I had to turn in my chair to see the soldier. I found him even more ugly than his speech hinted he would be.

The man ordered a beer and a whiskey. We returned to our game, myself and three of the cantina's regulars, only to find ourselves interrupted by the stranger.

"Deal me in," he said, dragging a chair to the table.

"We are not finished with the hand yet," said a German prospector. I found him well-spoken and polite, even when he was so inebriated he forgot how to speak either English or Spanish.

"You are now," said the stranger.

The German looked at the freedman to my left, who looked to the mestizo at my right, who looked at me. I shrugged, and the men grumbled a bit as we all laid down our hands and the German collected his winnings.

Now, your momma was never one for cheating. Your gran would not abide our use of magick to finish chores or avoid studying for our lessons, and we girls had learned early that the elders frowned upon magick that would break natural laws. As far as I was concerned, even my blind great-aunt Jeanne would be able to tell this brute had not had the same schooling. He was accustomed to acting however he wished because of his size. The scar running from his hairline over his eye socket and ending in the hollow of his cheek was testament to the fact someone had once tried to teach him a lesson and failed.

He sat himself down between the German and the mestizo, and though they made the room for him, it was for their own benefit rather than his.

Though I cannot recall with sharp detail how the first hand played out, I can recall the freedman won and the brute called him greasy, or else something to that effect. It was an effort for the rest of us not to laugh at the soldier, who grew more inebriated as the game went on but was holding it well enough. The freedman won the second hand as well, for which the rest of us would have rejoiced were it not for the uninvited player at the table.

"You mangy half-breed," the brute called him after draining his glass.

I was drawing a breath to speak when the mestizo and I locked eyes. In his I saw an admonition, and I understood this would run its course. Same as any other storm, all we could do was wait it out. So I held my tongue as the brute stood from the table to fetch another drink.

The rest of us continued slowly drinking our own beers. As the freedman shuffled the deck and started dealing out the hand, the brute wiped a line of foam from the whiskers on his top lip and sneered.

"What's taking you so long?" he asked. "They not teach you how to count on the plantation?"

Though the freedman paused in his dealing to fix the brute with a hard stare, he held his tongue. Gone was the friendliness of the banter, the lightness with which we teased each other from time to time. This man had no lightness in his heart.

The freedman won the hand he'd dealt, and the brute slammed a hand the size of a shank onto the tabletop. As I drew a breath the mestizo would have silenced, that hand left the table and shot out to grab the freedman by the forearm. Though he tugged, the freedman was unsuccessful in slipping the brute's grip. We had all seen the faded rope burns around both wrists, but the sight shocked the soldier.

"You a runaway?"

The freedman narrowed his eyes.

"What is this word?" the German asked.

"He means," the freedman said with an edge to his tone, "a runaway slave."

"Well, ain't you?" the soldier asked.

"No. I ain't."

I could not abide the brute's insults. This rotten-mouthed drunkard was allowed his malice because he was not sat at a table with men of violence, and I thought of a boy I had once known who terrorized a schoolyard for the same reason. He could get away with it, and so he had kept at it.

To snip a lock of his hair or infuse one of his personal effects with perfume would be too obvious, and so I had to improvise. I drew not on a practiced spell but rather one I had been concocting since he first insulted the German. In my mind, I had unleashed it after he insulted the mestizo, and that crack at the freedman was the spark I needed. I needed no spark to cheat at cards, but this was not about cheating, or cards.

As if summoned, another United States Army soldier stepped in out of the dust and the cloudless afternoon and stood a moment in the doorway. Your father would later attest to knowing I was the one he was looking for before he even stepped in from outside. Still, he spoke to the owner's son behind the bar before he did anything else. Though I was aware of him, I paid him no mind. Not even after Chimalli picked me out of a crowd of dusty, weathered men and said, "Yep, that'd be her over there."

It must have been then that the commanding officer entered. My attention was on the brute refusing to release the freedman's wrist. The freedman had himself braced against the table with his opposite hand, just as the brute had used his unoccupied one to slip from his boot a knife. Its edge glinted in the dusty light, and I began to murmur under my breath.

Helios, ire

Burn like fire

Five times I spoke the incantation below my breath. The handle grew too warm for the brute to hold, whereupon he buried the blade in the tabletop and stood with a roar. While the others had missed it, he had heard my chant. His eyes moved between his hand and my face.

"You're a goddamned WITCH," he said.

Where we were, the law was no good. The men at the table were grimy, their nails black from gunpowder and dirt and blood, their mouths kept clean by corn whiskey, and I had been listening to them tell stories for months by the time the army sent a couple of their men out to collect me. All three were on their feet and reaching for their own weapons in the time it took the newcomer to confirm he had found me. While the brute would come back to his senses, his pounding headache and blank memory offering him penance and absolution both, I would not be there to witness the reunion.

The newly arrived soldier was tall and young, with hair the color of copper and an earnest face I could tell was used to smiling, though there was no call for smiling at the moment we met. He walked right up to the brute, called him Mitchell, said he ought to put the knife away before he hurt himself.

"Lieutenant's on his way," he added. "If you're gonna be a drunk, do it at the bar."

To all of our surprise, the brute did as he was told and stalked off.

Once he had gone, the red-haired soldier turned to me and asked, "Miss, is your name Lilian MacPherson?"

I asked, "*¿Estoy detenida?*"

He laughed like I had told a joke and said, "You ain't under arrest. You are coming with us, though."

I told him I had to finish my hand first.

"Looks like you oughta fold that hand anyway," he said.

"She's cheating!" the brute yelled from the bar.

The freedman and the mestizo both groaned and began grousing to each other, while the German took off his hat and downed his beer.

Now that we were interrupted, I saw no point in doing anything other than what I did, which was roll my eyes and fold my hand and leave the cantina with the soldiers. Behind me, the brute continued to holler about witchery. I do not know what happened to him after I left, but I have no doubt the three gamblers and the bartender were able to dispatch him.

"I can take care of myself, you know," I said.

"No, actually," said the red-haired soldier's commanding officer, a taller and sturdier man who looked as if he had just stepped out of whatever academy produces men like him. "You can't. Matter of fact, we ought to have you arrested for assaulting a soldier."

The soldiers marched me not to the county jail but straight to the stagecoach station. Once we were aboard, they sat across from me talking and telling each other jokes, and I passed the early leg of the journey staring out the window and ignoring the both of them.

"You got good timing," the red-haired soldier said when dusk fell. I looked away from the landscape to find his fellow asleep beside him. I did not ask him what he meant, but he told me anyway. "A year or two earlier, Bird's Fort would've been abandoned. There'd be nothing out here but Comanche braves."

I held to my silence. We looked each other in the eye for a moment, I with my jaw set and he seeming far older than the nineteen or so years he was truly, and then he shook his head. Some time would pass before I would ask him what he had been thinking, then. At the time I just looked away, watching the wilds disappear and the next city bleed into its space.

"I never heard anyone called a witch before," he said.

I shrugged.

"Mighty powerful word to name a woman in public."

I shrugged again.

"Folks name what they don't understand as the work of the devil," I said. "Imagine the same goes for people that don't look like what they're used to." I paused and added, "Or maybe he just didn't like losing to a girl."

"I saw the three you were holding," he said. "If his were worse than that, I can see why he'd be sore."

We were ten days overland, at the time the longest ten days of my life, before we arrived at the roadhouse. What conversation passed during that time was often between the two soldiers, the older of the two inclined to speak of me as if I were not present and I to ignore him. Though the red-haired soldier attempted to make conversation between stageline stops, he abandoned the effort by the third day.

On the tenth day, the soldiers confirmed the address with the stagecoach driver and delivered me direct to the front porch.

I felt a stab of guilt when your gran came into sight, for she was not your gran then but only my momma, and my momma was standing out on the porch like she was expecting us.

My momma, whose skirt I had held tight to when I was still learning how to walk, who stood straight and unflinching with her aunts and her sisters in a circle formed of salt and sweat and whispered incantations when they thought the children were in bed. Whose words I would never interrupt, whose circle I would never break, because I thought I knew what it was to respect her. Whose corner of the Grand Library lay beneath a fine layer of dust, not because she was untidy but because it allowed her to track which books my heedless fingers had eased from the shelves. She wore a shawl around her thin shoulders, only the wind moving the hem on her dress and the ends of her hair. I would have preferred a cold reception to the pain I saw in her eyes.

I did not think she would embrace me in front of those soldiers, those men she did not know, but she did. She took me by the elbows and looked me up and down and then she wrapped me up in her arms like I was a child she had thought lost at the market. Nothing else in the world but me and her now that I was back.

Of course I squirmed against her. Not only were the soldiers standing right there looking but the door opened and out came my cousins Eva and Charlotte. They were not giggling at my embarrassment. They were giggling at the two men brung me home. Ma did thank them for returning me, and they did tip their hats when she invited them in for supper. They had to be getting back, though goat's head stew did sound lovely.

When my mother released me, I turned towards the soldiers and, though I drew a breath to speak, could think of nothing I wanted to say to either of them. The red-haired soldier met my gaze, and he gave me a lopsided smile I had no way of knowing would become familiar to me as the years went on.

And once they were nothing more than memory for the wind to take away, I told my mother I was sorry.

It was not a word any of us girls ever used much. My eldest cousin, Agnes, said it more than the rest of us combined, but she never meant it. I'm not sure I meant it, myself. This was my home and this was where my kin were, and though my momma loved me something fierce, I would not have left if my sense of belonging had been strong enough to overcome my sense of longing.

"Don't you dare apologize," my momma said. "The next time you go, you won't return. No sense saying you're sorry if you're going to do it again anyway."

The war in Mexico began in the spring of 1846, and so soon as it began, it took to chewing up soldiers fast as the army could send them, spitting them back out again. We saw it in the ones who returned, the permanent sunburns on their faces and hands, the faraway fixation in their eyes, on some unending horizon we girls could not see ourselves as we wiped down the tables and fetched them their beers. Ours was not a house of ill repute, as the God-fearing folks call them. My cousins and I did not sell our bodies to the men who passed through, though Agnes was fond of romancing men she fancied if they planned on staying in town for a spell.

I was not adventurous in the way Agnes was, at least not as far as my body was concerned. While she worked spells to make herself more attractive to a certain kind of man, I crushed aloe leaves and coated my hands and skin with their juice to protect me from just that kind of man.

Something about the anger in my bones, the lack of interest or attraction in my eyes when I looked straight into theirs, seemed to some men a challenge. It was not meant as such. The ones with half a brain in their skull flinched away from me when our eyes met, and that was just the way I preferred it.

"For not liking men, you sure spend enough time with them," said Eva from her place at the dressing table, where she brushed her hair. I was sitting on the edge of my bed, working the aloe juice into my cuticles.

"It ain't that I don't like men," I said. "I don't like drunks, or fools."

"That why you're always playing cards with them?"

"If they ain't got enough sense not to play cards with a teen-aged girl, who am I to tell them to go somewhere else? Train tickets are expensive."

"Cousin," she said with a laugh, "you are incorrigible."

"Besides," I said, "I like tall men, who are kind, and have eyes blue like soldiers' uniforms."

"Oh," said Eva, "you mean that man brought you home that time you ran away."

"No!" I said, which only made her laugh harder.

As retribution, I twirled my pointer finger in the air one, two, three times and then flexed all my fingers, as I would to toss powder at her. Her hairbrush caught in her mane, and her yelp of surprise followed me out of the room.

"Tangling my hair don't mean I'm wrong!"

Later that night I came in from a late venture hoping I could creep uninterrupted past the saloon to the second floor. From my room I had a view of the courtyard garden we tended throughout the day. On nights I felt my wanderlust too strong for sleep, I would sit up on the window seat staring out at the flowers planted among the milk thistle and ginger and aconite, and think of their petals soaking up the moonlight, and I would feel a kinship with them. If they pulled up their roots, they would die.

My thoughts were on my view of the garden as I climbed the stairs, but even so, Agnes's voice stopped my feet before I had time to process the words, protests against a man with a rough voice and rougher hands. I stopped halfway up the stairwell, then turned and hurried back into the corridor, lit by oil lamps and moonlight.

The man, who I had never seen before, had my older cousin against the wall, unable to move and unwilling to invoke magick to free herself. I was not. I was then several years on from the age I was when I first hexed Danny Chesterfield in the schoolyard, and I was twice as strong both in body and in spirit. When I grabbed the man by the shoulders and pushed him away from Agnes, I did so not with my hands but with the power of my mind. Fire is the element with which I have always felt a certain sort of kinship, but Fire would choke and die without Air, and it was Air that allowed me to knock the man back several steps. His shoulders hit the wall, hard, and gave me his attention. Whiskey had soured his breath and I could not tell whether the distance in his eyes was the fault of drink or the war. They widened, once, when he realized but for my cousin and I he was alone in the corridor. He did not notice when I plucked his wallet from his belt. He did notice when I snarled at him to get off of Agnes and get the hell out of the inn.

In spite of Agnes imploring me to let him be since he was going without any more fuss, I returned to the room I shared with her sister to retrieve a book of matches and a bottle of perfume. Luck or some other trickster must have been on my side, for Eva was not in our room at the time. Shushing Agnes on my way out the door, I followed the brute into the street. There I sprayed the wallet with the scent and intoned a spell whose words I will not record here, as it is one you will have to learn yourself. I ought to have done so indoors, or at least in the shadow where none would see me, but I did not. There are far too many *oughts* and *shoulds* in this story. They have no business in your spells. Look forward, my dear, not behind.

I was able to follow along after the brute and, cloaked by the spell whose intonation I have not recorded, walk right up to his door without alerting anyone to my presence. Or so I thought.

I left the wallet in front of his door and returned home to the inn, and the spell worked its way with him. Overnight his hips grew wide and his breasts full, his hair long and his skin soft. He walked with a lightness in his step he could not control, and his voice was soft, his moods given to sea changes. I skipped breakfast the next morning to crowd the window in childless Aunt Griselda's room, and was laughing into the palm of my hand when a shadow cut across the floor behind me.

"What have you done?" Eva asked.

"I don't know what you're talking about," I said.

"My perfume bottle's gone," she said, her tone grim. "I know you done something, Lily; I can feel it in the air. Last night I dreamed they were burning you. What've you done?"

"Take it easy," I said as I climbed down from the window seat. "I ain't done nothing that can't be undone."

"That's of no concern to them," she said. "You know how easy men scare. You may as well have turned him into a goat."

"Do you know that one?" I asked. "Would you teach me?"

Eva rolled her eyes and did not answer, knowing well when I was gnashing my teeth.

By the next evening the brute had fingered me as the one who hexed him, and all of the men who had seen me disappear on the street had had time to work themselves into a posse. The tavern downstairs was full as ever, weary travelers and riverboat conductors looking to stand still for a few hours keeping the taps running and the aunties bustling, but it was like my cousin had said—my hex had left a stain in the air.

I succeeded in my task of keeping distance between myself and my mother, and though I did not see her the rest of the day, I did feel the prickling of magick that was the grandmothers and the eldest cousins casting a protective circle around the property. No one with ill intent in their hearts could cross the threshold of the place, but none of my kin thought to ward the house against my leaving.

I stepped out of the inn just before sundown, intending to go on about my evening in spite of what was gathering outside, and in doing so found a group of ten men waiting for me, with more stopping what they were doing to see what would happen. Those ten were armed with ropes and torches they intended to light, not for brilliance but for burning.

Your gran had seen me leave the house, and set down the glass she was filling to rush out after me, to fling wide the doors leading to the inn's front porch and step between me and the posse. I still do not know whether what happened next came by coincidence or by some Work of my cousins seeking to keep me safe. But at that moment, with everything else going down, an army company rode into town on their horses. They were on their way to the Mexican front and like as not intending to stop at the barracks just outside of town for the night. Instead of rest, they found a group of men looking to string up a witch.

The posse was in no state to take on a company of soldiers, and while the others dismounted, a soldier with a corporal medic's insignia rode up to me and held out his arm. I was preparing to run when I looked up from the hand to glimpse the face. His cap hid his red hair, but I recognized the eyes in an instant. It was the soldier who had escorted me back from Texas a few years earlier. He had earned some stripes since the last time I saw him, but unlike the other noncommissioned officers, he did not wear a sword.

"Why am I not surprised?" he asked, with a lopsided grin that I answered with a scowl. He held out his hand more firmly and said, "I'm trying to help you, come on now."

So I grabbed Corporal Callahan's forearm and, rather than allow him to haul me into the saddle behind him, used him as a ballast.

I was dressed for an evening of cleaning up slopped beer and climbing cellar stairs to fetch more gin, not for riding horses, and I was quite certain the animal would buck me if afforded the opportunity. Once I was astride the saddle, I latched my arms around the corporal's waist so tight I heard the wind shoot out of him.

"Easy," he said, and started the horse to trotting. "I ain't gonna let you fall."

"The hell with you," I said. "I ain't gonna let me fall."

Aside from squeezing through crowds of gamblers and drunks, or the rare embrace I tolerated from an uncle or a male cousin, I had never been so close to a man before either. To be frank, they were stranger to me than horses were. Upon inhaling, I found the corporal did not reek of tobacco or whiskey, as I was expecting. Nor was I transported by his nearness or his scent. Whatever stories Agnes had been telling us younger girls about being around men were just that—stories.

"Where in the hell are you taking me?" I asked.

"You got a mouth on you," he said.

"Where? Tell me."

"We're gonna ride around for a bit and then double back. Lieutenant Ness has got a way with people. I'm sure the mob'll be long gone by the time we get there."

"Well, bully for Lieutenant Ness," I said.

This too made the corporal laugh, which caused a curious flush to blossom in my chest and find its way into my cheeks. I had no interest in charming or impressing this gentleman, but something beyond my control occurred when I heard him smile. All I knew was I wanted this ride to end so I could return to the inn and accept the punishment awaiting me.

So I kicked his boots out of the stirrups and replaced them with my own. In the moment I had earned by startling him, I sent his boot and the spur attached to it into the horse's flank. As the animal began to canter, the man who would become your father asked me whether I wanted to hold the reins too.

I loosed an unladylike snort but gave no other reply. To our left was the Mississippi River, to the right the bloodied western sky. I was growing accustomed to the quiet of the evening when the corporal spoke again.

"You know, this is the second time I've saved you after someone called you a witch and said they were going to kill you."

"You call that saving?" I asked. "I'd been just fine without you."

"Is that so? And what's your pa think of all this trouble you keep getting into?"

"How should I know? I never knew him. Got this far without his help and don't need yours, neither."

"Well, you got ample kin from what I've seen."

"What do you know about it?"

"Absolutely nothing."

I could not see his face, but I knew his smirk was gone.

"That why you joined the army?" I asked.

"I wanted to save people, and the army needed medics. I make it through the war, I get to be a doctor." I heard his grin return. "Besides, coal mining ain't in my blood."

"Too bad. Your face would look better with soot on it."

He laughed, and though I would have denied it at the time, so did I.

"Why'd you want to be a doctor?" I asked.

He held his tongue a moment, and I let him.

"Surmise it's my own way of getting back at Death for taking my kin. Even the score, or something."

We rode in silence, the angry, fatherless witch and the kinless corporal with an account to settle with the Reaper. As I look on you now, I realize that was the moment I first began to pine for your father.

By the time we finished the circuit around the waterfront, the corporal's brothers in arms had cleared the front porch and the street of both lynchers and bystanders, and the only folks left outside were a tall man wearing the single-bar insignia of a second lieutenant and your gran, eyeing us like she knew what was coming. Maybe she did. She waited for me to dismount before she thanked the lieutenant and the corporal kindly, and she waited for them to trot off to reconvene with their men before she took me by the arm and marched me into the Library. I would have preferred one of Aunt Griselda's tongue lashings compared to your gran's punishment, but I learned.

The next morning, I and my cousin Charlotte were sat in the courtyard garden while the rest of the household cleaned up after breakfast. My task was to restore a fallow section of garden. I was to do this not with my hands but with my Will. Charlotte was sat crafting a chain from the daisies she grew by passing her bare palm over the grass beside her. Aside from the occasional rustling of the breeze through the trees, her humming was the only sound in the yard. I was unable to convince even a blade of grass to emerge from the dirt and fixing to give up when the both of us heard the jangling of spurs from within the house.

My cousin kept working at her chain, but I dusted off my hands and found my feet, holding my shoulders square so as to seem taller than my due. Even with the heels on my boots, I was the shortest of my kin. Stood before a man full grown, I aimed to carry myself like a woman.

"We are bound for Fort Smith," said Corporal Callahan, and he kept his hat in his hands though we were out of doors and the sun was beginning to overtake the eastern sky. "I wanted to make sure you ain't found more trouble since I last saw you."

"You'd like that, wouldn't you?" I asked.

"Not at all," he said. "In fact, I hope if ever our paths cross again, it is to wave and say hello, and if you and I decide to stop and chat awhile, I will find it a pleasant change of both pace and peril."

Though I had no desire to fall for him, I desired less that this man would think his absence affected me. So I stuck out my right hand and did not react when the false certainty in the gesture provoked him to smile and clasp palms.

"Farewell, Corporal," I said, giving his hand several firm shakes.

"See ya around, Miss MacPherson," he said.

He let himself back inside the house, and I returned to my place in the dead patch of garden. No sooner had I smoothed my skirts and breathed in deep the smell of nothingness, the garden dirt needing blood and bone to live, than Charlotte laughed at something the flowers were whispering to her.

"You're gonna marry him," she said.

"The hell I am," I said.

"Look," she said, and held up the necklace she had been weaving as I conversed with the army doctor.

"What am I looking at?" I asked.

"These two right here," she said, and pointed to a knot in the necklace. "They tied themselves together."

"You sure that don't mean you and Thomas Hume are gonna run off and have a bunch of babies?"

"Thomas Hume is afraid of me," she said. "That one ain't afraid of you."

That was not enough to convince me of anything, not at the time, but my heart must have been yearning towards lighter things. As I passed my palm over the dead patch of earth, the dry gray dirt churned and rippled. When it settled again, it was rich and dark and good. It did not turn to dust when I sank my fingers into it. I pulled them out again, and the damp soil clung to my skin, and from out of the holes grew wildflowers.

Your father sent me a telegraph upon his arrival in New Orleans. It read:

Bound for Veracruz. First time aboard ship. Think you would like it in N.O. Stay out of trouble. Matthew.

Sensing he had little else to lift his spirits, I began to write letters to him. I did not write often, and I did not write much. From where I sat in my dry, quiet bedroom, this soldier had traveled farther and freer than I ever had. He was where my thoughts went when I allowed them to wander during lessons and meals.

Months passed before I received a proper letter in the post from the army doctor. He answered the questions I had posed in my own correspondences, and asked a few of his own. I resisted the notion of allowing him anything other than distant friendship, though of course my cousins found the affair romantic and needled me for details soon as a new letter arrived, dusty and battered. Naming the sensation was impossible at the time, but my cousins kept on with their needling, and it occurred to me that I, in my seventeen years of life, had never felt understood until I began corresponding with your father.

As that occurrence came to me, so did its companion—that each span of time between letters might be the final silence, that I would never know if he had died because so far as the army was concerned, I was nothing to him.

One morning, I took a long walk out of the city and into the quarry fields that lay west of the Missouri River to search

for a rare stone. Looking back, I could have spoken to my
mother of my need and asked for her assistance. But admitting
to her I feared for the safety of a man I only truly knew through
correspondence would have meant admitting it to myself. So I
went alone.

The books in the Library named quartz as a stone of protection, one that would serve best as a talisman rather than a
spell. Different colors were meant for different purposes. Rose
for protection during pregnancy and childbirth, smoky for protection against ill will, blue for protection against fear. Though
I will admit to being a brash girl who let her hot blood drive
her more often than her head, in this instance I was not seeking to punish another for what they had done to me or mine. I
was seeking to keep from danger the man who would be your
father. I needed amethyst.

Dusk did not come until late in the evening, but just before
it did come and steal away the light with it, I found glinting far
off along an unused trail a suggestion of what I needed. I knelt
in the dirt and began to brush away the sand with my fingers.
The amethyst's edges were worn down by salt and storms and
time, and I sat back on my haunches to consider its utility. The
leather cord I had chosen wrapped around the stone as if they
were both of them incomplete until this moment, and it was
long enough that when I tied it around my neck, the stone lay
flat against my breastbone.

Once it was done, I secreted the charm beneath my dress. I knew the spell would work if I kept my thoughts on the corporal until I removed the charm. Though I allowed myself to feel foolish for a few seconds before beginning the long walk back to town, after that moment of reproach, I thought only of the man to whom I would mail the necklace in the morning.

Thirteen days after the United States of America claimed victory over the United Mexican States, Eva and Charlotte chased me into the bedroom and onto my bed, testing the limits of the aging frame as they laughed and jostled.

"How am I supposed to read it with your elbow in my face?" I asked Eva.

"Open it, open it!" Charlotte said.

"I'm trying!" I said.

Once I had the letter free and open in my hands, I held my breath for not knowing what it would say. I was prepared for bad news, to learn the army was moving him to the desert, to the ocean, someplace I would never see him again. Or worse, that he was going to one of the big cities back east, engaged to be married to a coal baron's daughter rather than squander his time on the half-breed daughter of a roadhouse matron.

Eva squealed and clung to my arm as I read aloud what he wrote.

Dear Miss MacPherson,

It is with great relief that I write to inform you of the 6th Infantry's orders to return north to Jefferson Barracks, Missouri, so soon as we break camp in the morning. Though I will very much miss the sun, the sand, and the occasional scorpion nesting in my boot, we are coming home. The war is over. I have every confidence you and I will meet again in St. Louis, and feel it is not too much to hope I will not have to compete with an inebriate or posse for your attention this time.

Yours, Matthew J. Callahan

I had spent hours in the Library seeking spells that would force the days to proceed more quickly, or quell the ache in my chest when I thought of him. Speaking with my cousins did nothing but confirm my suspicions: that his red hair meant he would be fierce and loyal; that his pulling me onto his horse was the most romantic act ever recorded in the history of the MacPherson women; that my talisman had protected him from the perils across the Rio Grande.

Our mothers sensed mischief, they having been teenaged girls themselves once, but it was not until the last letter telling of the soldiers' return to Missouri that your gran called me into the tavern before we opened the doors for business. She handed me a clean rag and put me to work drying champagne flutes while she studied me.

"You're flushed," she said.

"I'm not," I said.

"It's a man."

"It's not."

"Dear heart," your gran said, "I'm old, not blind. I've read your cups, and even if I hadn't, it's all over your face. You think you're in love."

As I write to you now, my dear, I wonder what she would have said if I had asked her what she saw when she read my cups. I suppose she would have lied, or at least kept what she had seen to herself. Divination is a power I have not studied as have some of my kin, but those who have devoted their studies to its mastery can appreciate the burden foreknowledge places on them.

Nothing she could have told me would have changed what happened. I was too stubborn to do anything but what I was fated to do. Your gran knew that. She knew me better than anyone, at least before your father came along.

4

IT WAS A COLD WINTER'S DAY when your father returned to me.

The snow was falling steady, and he had a dusting of white upon his cap and shoulders as he stood in the doorway. His insignia had gained another stripe since we had seen each other, which I believe made him a sergeant, but it was his eyes I noticed before his dress. They had aged. The sun had freckled his skin, and I would see later that it had lightened his hair. He was as I remembered him, but leaner, rawer. Otherwise whole and unharmed, his appearance brought a flush to my cheeks. I blamed the elements.

"I'm not accustomed to meeting you in such circumstances," he said.

"In the snow?" I asked.

"Without sign of peril," he said.

"Seems to me the war has fogged your recollection," I said. "All you did was arrest a winning hand of brag and take me for a ride on what I recall to be a flea-ridden horse."

"I wore the necklace," he said.

"You did?"

"Of course," he said. "It's hard to find quality jewelry for men in wartime." I laughed. He went on, "I'm leaving in a week's time to attend medical college in Illinois."

As I could not predict what he would say next, I held my tongue.

He went on, "I was hoping you would join me."

"In what capacity?" I asked. "As your jeweler?"

"As my wife," he said.

Your mother was a fool, my dear. I was young, and I was not half as wise as I thought I was. What your father and I had was strong enough to survive in the middle of a desert, atop a mountain in the Arctic, and I let a city drive us towards his grave. We could have stayed in Chicago. We could have returned to St. Louis. We could have gone anywhere in the world besides damned De Soto, but I—

I am getting ahead of myself.

Your gran took the news of my intention to run away with the army doctor as well as anyone would have, which is to say she neither cursed him with impotence and baldness nor did she and her sisters summon natural disasters and mechanical failure to impede our journey north. She helped me pack, which is more than I could have expected from her. My cousins were beside themselves with joy and jealousy both. I promised to write.

Were your father intending to stay in St. Louis, I imagine he would have courted me through the winter, that we would have wed come springtime, during the revival and awakening of the world. According to tradition, springtime is the only acceptable time for a witch to perform the union ritual, and I could not wait so long to join your father. In three weeks' time he'd accepted his discharge from service and packed his bags and come to collect me.

In ways we had not in our letters, your father and I spoke of the future on the trip north. It was a pleasure to be able to sit beside him, to explore the lines on the palm of his hand as he spoke of looking forward to teaching medicine rather than practicing it.

If I had valued our future as much as my own freedom, I would not be writing you this letter. Your father would be alive to tell you of our time in Chicago.

I imagine he would tell you of how we stepped off the steamboat into a windy January afternoon, how I held my spine straight and my chin up though the cold and the air brought water to my eyes, and I to your father's side. How he held an arm around my shoulders to protect me from the wind as the porter loaded our bags into the carriage. How I remained tucked against him for the duration of the ride from the ferry landing to the university.

I would like to think he was excited to have me with him as we dragged our belongings inside the looming gray terraced house where faculty and their families lived. He would not have told you of what we did that night, after we had finished putting the place together so it began to resemble our own home and agreed without speaking that we would sleep in the same bed.

If your father were still alive, he would tell you that the next morning, a Monday, he and I bundled up against the wind and made our way to the city's hall. I was nervous, as I knew several states had laws against whites marrying outside of their race and I knew Illinois still forbade whites from marrying blacks.

It was the first of many times I would fear for our safety, and the safety of the children I had begun to hope of having. It was the first of many times I felt I had betrayed the father I never knew when I claimed to be white. All the clerk cared to see was our birth certificates and our proof of address, and he was satisfied with what your father showed him. That your father's army discharge papers were in the stack must have helped. The clerk barely looked at me throughout the transaction.

Your father's hand was steady as he signed his name to the certificate of marriage. Mine shook. I was not quite nineteen years old, and was excited and scared. After it was done and the pen returned to the clerk, your father took my hand in his, and the shaking ceased.

We never discussed a ceremony. Many times in my young life, I had witnessed a union ceremony at the roadhouse. They were often conducted on the nights of a full moon, and they required blood, as most difficult tasks do. The women in our family do not join themselves to men who are weak, or hungry for power, or unable to accept that the Christian Bible is a story, not a stone tablet handed down from their God himself. Witches pray to no god, and honor only the earth and the powers on this earth. Contracting with spirits on the other side, I believe, is what has led to the formation of those terrible things man calls religions.

If your father and I had stayed in St. Louis, we would have stood before the rest of the MacPherson family and their kin and recited our vows not to our witnesses but to each other. We would have cut each other's palms with a dagger used only for such a ceremony. We would have performed, in our own room with the door closed, a ritual to ensure our fertility, and your father would have been recognized as kin to the MacPherson family.

This was how I chose to exercise my own freedom—by living among those who would cower or worse if they knew of the things I did in the light of day, and by binding myself to the man I chose not with blood but with ink.

Your father would tell you I was not happy in Chicago, that we did not have so much as a palmful of dirt to call a yard and I could not make use of the sloped rooftop. He would tell you, fondly I believe, of how I attempted to grow herbs in boxes on the windowsills, how I could not rely on nature because we did not get much sunlight in the winter months so I touched them often, sang to them often, carried on conversations with them often.

He would not tell you of the first argument he and I ever had. I will. I was wrong.

We were walking together on a damp afternoon. Students on bicycles rang their bells as they hurried past, and groups of men wearing white coats and stern expressions passed us by from time to time. I paid them no mind. I was listening to your father tell a story of a spectacle that had occurred in the operating theater that morning when I reached out to dance my fingertips over some sleeping vines clinging death-tight to the side of a lecture hall.

The vines, or at least the few I touched, rustled as if some live creature had awakened beneath them, and bulbs of pink and purple burst forth and blossomed. Your father jumped as if a shot had fired, and though he had known what I was capable of, having seen it in the windowsill garden and suspected it from the obsidian glass and the altar and all the other strange things that made our flat a home, I also know he was scared. Not of me. For me.

He reached across my body to grab my wrist, and I looked around to see more than a few bystanders staring at me.

"Walk faster," he said in a low voice he had never used before and never would again.

I did not speak again the entire way back to our flat, and he did not release my wrist. I felt as if he were dragging a disruptive child home from church, and was both ashamed and angry. Once the door was locked and his hands were freed, we faced each other.

"What were you thinking?" he asked.

"I wasn't," I said. "It isn't as if I can control it."

"Surely you can! Don't you understand the danger you put yourself in when you do things like that?"

"This is America," I said. "There are no witch hunters in America."

"Oh, no? Why don't you ask the good people of Salem, Massachusetts, about witch hunters?"

Your father took my crossing my arms over my chest for agreement. I went to him then, tucked myself against his chest, and wrapped my arms around his waist. If I had known, I would have forced myself to be happy. I would have done so many things different if I had known what would happen. But our future was nowhere in sight then. It was just your father and me in a cold and crowded city, and I promised him I would be more careful.

For the next several years, your father would tell you, he and I tried for a baby.

Your father was afraid for my safety, and with good reason. I could only imagine what would happen to a child in this city, a girl child who amused herself by braiding a horse's mane with only her thoughts or lighting and extinguishing oil lamps in shop windows with the blink of an eye, reading strangers' thoughts and announcing them to all in earshot. We would have to remain indoors until she was old enough to control herself. We were a long way from St. Louis.

So I grew, among the other herbs, sprigs of wild carrot, or bishop's lace. After lying with your father, I would chew the seeds. It is most effective if taken as a tincture for seven days after, but we were newly wed and thought of ourselves as such for years afterwards. I do not believe he suspected. I believe he thought we would become parents when the time was right.

On a calm evening in June of 1855, your father returned home from the medical college with his usual mass of papers and books tucked inside his satchel, holding a telegraph in his hand. He all but hummed with anticipation as he turned my attention from my spellbook to kiss me.

"What's that?" I asked.

"We're expecting a guest," he said. "My old commanding officer."

"For how long?"

"A weekend," he said. "Maybe a bit longer. He says he has news."

"Splendid," I said though I did not mean it.

I cleaned the guest bedroom, as we had taken to calling the room that ought to have been our children's had your father's bride not been selfish and stupid. Opening the windows to blow away the dust and burning white sage to clear the energy in the room was as much for my sake as for our guest's. Your father picked him up from the train station, and I began preparing dinner. On a normal evening your father was the one who cooked, as my green thumb did nothing to assist me in culinary efforts, but this evening was not normal.

The men were laughing at some old story as they came up the stairs, a story that continued even after your father unlocked the door and allowed them both entry. Their boots clomping in the entryway was a sound to which I had yet to grow accustomed, as our home only ever admitted your father and me, or your father and a few of his colleagues from time to time. Not soldiers.

Lieutenant Henry Ness was a tall white man, taller than your father and built solid. In those days he did not wear a beard, nor had his brown hair begun to turn silver. It was blond from the time he had spent out west, and the tanned quality of his skin made him appear older than he was. He walked with a limp. That told me what his stature had not, what neither he nor your father would. In most circles it is considered poor manners to read a person's health when shaking their hand for the first time, but none of my kin were around to take me to task for doing just that. Ness left the army not by choice but because he had taken an arrow to the hip. It would take time and resilience for him to ride a horse without agony again.

"Li Lian," Ness said correctly for the first and last time, "it is a pleasure and an honor to be a guest in your home."

After dinner the men smoked tobacco pipes and I cleaned up. The hour grew quite late, but our minds were clear and sharp. Your father was prepared for Ness's proposal. I was not.

Ness said, "Matt, I know you've got a real bright future here, but it doesn't take a bright man to teach. You get what I'm saying? The country's bigger than it used to be, and it's safer to move out west than it was two, three years ago. All the same, it's hard as hell to find someone as intelligent and dedicated as you are actually out there practicing medicine. A lot of places don't even have a doctor. You should see what happens to those places come wintertime, or when a sickness breaks out. I've been through some ghost towns in my time—you'd think the Indians had had at them. Wasn't the Indians. It was folks trying to start a town without any sort of law in place."

The question hung in the air, and Ness answered it.

"Nebraska."

"Nebraska," your father repeated.

"Yep. De Soto, in particular. They need a sheriff, and they're going to need themselves a doctor."

I excused myself and began preparing for bed then, my thoughts getting away from me. The word Nebraska brought to mind open plains and tall grass and houses spread so far apart it wouldn't matter if the trees I touched became heavy with fruit when they ought to have dried up, or if I walked outside without shoes and brought up wildflowers in my wake. Chicago was a cage. Out in the wilds was where my heart wanted to be.

More than the wilds, though, I wanted to be where Matthew was. If he had wanted to stay in Chicago, I would have made my heart want the same thing. I would have given him the strength to tell his old friend no, and I would have stopped chewing wild carrot seeds to keep our children from growing inside of me. In time I would have learned to love that ugly city, to like wearing gloves like a proper lady, to mind my tongue when I was speaking to the other mothers when our babies were old enough to need walking to school. If that was what he wanted, he would still be alive right now.

He wanted to go to De Soto. He told me so when he and Ness finally quit jawing sometime around one in the morning and he climbed into bed with me. My back found his chest though I was still half-asleep. In his arms, I thought his words made sense.

"I think we're moving to the Nebraska Territory," he said.

And I said, "I think you're right, my love."

5

IT WOULD BE A LIE to say your father and I had no way of knowing the three highwaymen were set to come the night they came.

The three years that passed after our arrival in De Soto blurred together. I grew my garden on the land behind our cabin, and we wanted for little. You had already quickened, but my belly had not begun to show, at least not to anyone unfamiliar with my body. If it were up to your father, I would have stayed home the rest of the year and turned the place into a nest. We were happy, and I felt no portend in the wind.

I had been standing sideways before the mirror, guessing at how much longer we would have to wait for you to arrive without turning to clairvoyant magick, when the glass shimmered the way still waters move when disturbed by a pebble or an adventurous fish. An image of your gran appeared before me. Though she startled me, I was pleased to see her. I would have told her so, but I could no more converse with her image than I could have with a telegram. That was not the sort of spell she had Worked. When the message finished, I dressed and went out to the kitchen to join your father.

"Ma tells me three highwaymen stopped at the inn a fortnight past," I said.

"How's she know they were highwaymen?"

By then your father ought to have known the answer: she just knew. She never revealed how. She knew the men's faces and she knew their names. It may have been she saw their intentions smudged on the glassware they left behind, or hiding in the shadows they cast upon the dusty floors. Perhaps it wasn't magick at all. They could have got themselves loosened up on your great-auntie Griselda's corn whiskey while your gran and Auntie Lucinda sat themselves awhile, listening and laughing at what the men revealed.

"Let me guess," said Matthew. "She just knows?"

I planted a kiss on his forehead, which did nothing to smooth his worry lines.

According to your gran's message, the three were headed west through the Nebraska Territory. They had spoken of a debt owed, and they brought with them no good omen.

"What'd she say they looked like?" your father asked.

"She didn't," I said.

"How are we supposed to know it's them, then?"

"If we see strange men numbering three, I reckon we'll know."

"This is Nebraska. Strange men abound."

Your father had used sage and rosemary to season the eggs and potatoes he cooked for breakfast. He asked before he did it, knowing the uses I had for white sage. The sage used for seasoning is not the sage we use for cleansing. They are different families of herbs altogether, and it is the white sage you do not want to give away or ingest. White sage burns well and the burning does away with darkness and malevolence, but it will make a body sick if taken by mouth. Telling the difference is easy even in the dark. Cooking sage is a green gray and smells of mint, while white sage is silver gray and smells of nothing though it glows like smoke. Never share the white sage with any but your cousins, and do not judge harshly the man you choose for thinking them the same.

After breakfast, your father and I went ahead as if the day were the same as the one come before, but I know the message nagged at him. Your father knew well enough that our magick was real and if it offered a warning, he would do well to heed it. He went into town to open his office for his patients while I stayed behind to tend our garden. It was a quiet day, and a fine one.

When your father returned that afternoon, I was still working in the garden, my hands painted with fertile dirt and crushed sage. Streaks of it stained my face from my fighting with the breeze over an errant strand of hair. Your father asked if I was making a charm, and I told him yes.

"What for this time?" he asked.

"Unity," I said. "So long as the poppet I make remains intact, it will keep us and the baby safe."

"It will?"

"Mm hmm."

"Well now," he said, kneeling down and brushing back my hair with his hands, "that's my job, ain't it?"

What happened next, my dear, I will keep for myself. It would be the last time we ever lay together.

That evening, your father and I took a light supper and sat out on the porch to watch the sunset. I liked to watch the sun set and hold your father's hand while it did so, and once darkness fell we bolted the doors and lit a single oil lamp. As we prepared for bed, I heard horses on the path leading to our front porch.

Neither of us spoke. I peered out the front window and saw two men on horseback. One of the men dismounted and helped the other, who was slumped forward against the horse's neck. The injured man leaned on his companion as they hobbled towards our front door.

On an ordinary evening, I would not have hesitated to open the door to help someone in need, as your father was the only physician for miles around and we had grown accustomed to folks calling on him at all hours of the night. But the bad omen and memory of your gran in the mirror stayed my hand. Rather than open the door, I peeked through the curtain.

The uninjured man was short, like as not in his fourth decade. Though he was small and his dark hair silvering, I knew by the way he carried himself that if he got it into his mind to be violent, the violence would come to him easy as breathing. His eyes were squinted as if he were sentenced to walk the rest of his days through a dust storm, and he wore a powder horn on his belt, a bandana around his neck. On the back of his right hand was an old brand. I do not think he was cruel by choice, but a life of cruelty had made him so. Even before he spoke, I recognized him as Mexican.

His injured companion would have stood as tall as your father were he standing, but he was not. He was now crumpled on the front porch, all sinew and callouses. Hair the same color as the hay we fed the horses and drenched in sweat. His skin, drained of blood on account of injury and pain, would have been pale even in broad daylight.

Behind me your father was gathering up his medical bag, and I took comfort in hearing him. I opened the door only a crack, enough to confirm what I saw through the window.

The younger of them was drenched not only in sweat but in blood, his shirt and right leg dark and shimmering with it. The stench of tobacco smoke and iron sweat and lathered horses clung to them. They both wore revolvers at their waists, and the older man wore a rifle slung across his back. The younger man's injuries eclipsed these signs of danger.

"We need a doctor for his leg," said the older man. "We hear there is one here."

I looked over the Mexican's shoulder, where two horses were tied to the fence. I tried to scent a trap on the wind, but all I could smell was injury and necessity. Without medical attention, the younger man would die.

Though my bones told me to stay rooted, I stepped out of the way and held the door open for them. Your father hurried out of the bedroom then with his bag, his shirtsleeves rolled up to his elbows, and without another moment's hesitation helped the Mexican carry his companion towards the dining table. I shut the door behind them and went into the pantry to fetch another lamp.

When the wounded man's body landed on the table, he screamed in pain and fear both, and I paused to listen before I came back out with an armful of clean rags, a bucket, and another lamp. A bullet had pierced the younger man's belly, and his leg was lacerated. Someone had tied a belt above the wound.

"Who put the tourniquet on?" your father asked.

"I did," the Mexican said.

"When?"

He removed a pocket watch from the vest he wore beneath his riding coat. Blood from an earlier consultation had stained the pewter casing.

"Three hours ago," said the Mexican. "Just before sundown."

Until my last breath I will remember that your father met my eyes then, and we spoke without speaking.

You can go, his eyes said.

I want to stay, mine said.

Are you sure? his asked.

Yes, mine answered.

So your father took up a place at the wounded man's side and examined the doomed leg. The bullet had lodged itself between the bottom of his rib cage and his right hipbone. Not a fatal shot, but as your father opened his shirt and exposed the wound, the smell of perforated bowels rose up out of it. I stood quiet and sure at your father's side and watched him cut away the wool to expose the leg, which was a far worse sight than the laceration I had imagined it to be when I first laid eyes on him. The bones above and below the knee had snapped into stakes and driven themselves through the flesh, twisting and tearing. Unconsciousness would have been a mercy for a man surviving such an injury, but this man was still conscious, and he lifted his head from the table to look down at the mess made of his leg before he swore and let his head fall back with a bang.

I can count on one hand the number of people for whom I would perform the ritual necessary to salvage flesh mangled so badly. It calls for blood and spit and pain, for the caster to grind up this mixture into ginger root and distilled spirits and to pray to the patient's ancestors not to light the hearth yet, for the patient has more steps to take on this earth. When performing magick that impacts the flesh, I find it necessary to call upon the departed family of the afflicted. They have the greatest hope of steering the living away from disaster. On this point your gran and I have never agreed. She believes the dead envy the living. You will find your own way of magick, and have your own arguments with her.

I knew the Work I could do to save it, and I knew the cost would be great. But he was not my blood, and some warning voice in the back of my mind echoed my mother's.

I could have read the future in the blood slicks wrung out of a linen rag into the bottom of a bucket. Magick is a tool, but I refuse to let it be a shackle. At the time, the choice I made appeared to be right. I have heard tell of witches who possess the power to turn back the clock and make a different choice, but their power extends only so far and the toll exacted is steeper than continuing on in spite of the misstep. I wish I could say I do not regret the path I took, but here I am looking back at the path and the damage done. There can be no undoing what was done without knowing what lay ahead.

Your father saw the leg and I saw the leg and the Mexican saw the leg. When your father asked what happened, they looked each other in the eye.

"Comanche," said the Mexican in a voice that sounded like sand and cheap whiskey.

"Comanche?" your father asked.

"Other side of the mountains. They fired on us, and his horse fell on his leg, and we fled."

We had not seen the Comanche around those parts the entire time we had lived in the Nebraska Territory. I thought of you again and I know you do not remember how I rubbed my belly, but I did.

"That tourniquet saved his life," said your father, "but the rest of the leg is dying already. If I don't take it off, he's liable to bleed to death. I can try to patch him up, sure, get him back on his horse, but that knee won't heal right and you might well run into trouble. Where'd you say you all were heading?"

"I didn't."

Your father cut me a glance and the younger man was no wiser for it, breathing fast and concerned with his own suffering as he was, but the older man had laid his hands on the table, heedless of the blood, a patient expression on his face.

"What are you saying, Doc?" the wounded man asked.

"I'm saying if I don't remove the leg, you're going to die."

The younger man began to cry, and in spite of my mistrust I found myself taking pity on him.

"You're not cutting off his leg," said the older man.

Your father said, "If I don't, the rot will spread to the rest of his body."

At that, your father put a hand on my elbow and turned me away from the table. In a quiet voice he told me he wanted the leg gone before extracting the bullet lodged in the man's gut.

No point digging it out if taking off the leg would kill him, and the bullet would be a smaller pain compared to the mangled limb. Even with the Mexican's help, I would not be able to hold still a man thrashing against amputation.

Without saying it aloud, we both knew someone who could help us, if he had not started drinking at noon. When you spend enough time with another person, you get to where your thoughts and theirs are bound together as cords in a rope.

Your father said, "Oh, no. Not him."

I said, "We need him."

"To do what? Disinfect the wound with his breath?"

"You know anyone else who'll help lop off a man's leg on such short notice?"

What tales I had heard tell of the butcher were of the same quality as the ones they told about me, I suspect. That he had himself a lucrative business back east collecting money and keeping his mouth shut when men and murderers brought bodies belonging to their victims to his farm in upstate New York. That he fed the corpses to his pigs, that sometimes the corpses weren't quite corpses yet. That his wife left him because she got to where she could discern no difference between the squealing of the pigs and the screaming of men being eaten alive. A ghoulish tale and one I suspected soon as I heard it to be false, but even false stories have a dash of truth to them.

"Be careful," your father said.

It is important to know your father and I married for strength and unity. My spirit met his spirit and they said to each other, *Yes, I remember you, we've met before and we will meet again.* Neither of us believed in sin or impurity, but that did not mean we did not believe in virtue and justice. We shared in each other's lives to make a new one, and when I walked out the door that night, I felt no premonition to tell me his would end upon my return.

I would have stayed, if I had. I should have stayed.

At night, the skies over the plains are clear and speckled bright with stars. The moon was a sickle blade that night and growing thinner. A cunning moon. I had little light by which to see, and I carried a lantern with me along the path leading to the town's main street.

Ours was a commerce town, growing fast and promising to support what businesses came out of it, but most folks just passed through on their way to something better. It was no trouble to walk from our cabin at the edge of town to the butcher's shop a mile or so down the lane. The post office and the general store and the miller had closed their windows against darkness and drunkards both. If not for the absence of clouds and the mildness of the temperature, I would have thought a storm to be looming. The air all but crackled with anticipation, the way it does before the lightning comes.

As I approached the butcher's shop, I saw a light still burning in a rear window, where it stood to reason Roger Hawking took his meals and slept. Having never been to his living quarters before, I was not of a mind to invite myself around back in search of an entrance, so I walked up the steps and pounded on the front door hard as I could. I heard nothing within and assumed he had not heard me, so I left the porch and went around the building. We met each other in the alleyway.

The butcher stumbled around the corner with his rifle pointed at me, though I doubt he could see straight enough to hit the side of the building.

"We ain't open," he said in a growl.

"Quit pointing that thing at me," I said, raising the lantern to my face. "It's me."

"Lilian?" He lowered the muzzle. "The hell you doing out here? Ain't you know what time it is?"

With the breeze blowing as it was, I could smell the state the butcher had worked his body into, and I thought then I ought to see him back inside and return home to your father. Tell him Hawking was in a bad way and of no use to anyone, that we could remove the leg without him if it was that important. There is not much to men's bodies. Theirs are simpler machines than a woman's, needing only to support one life within the span of their own, and at the time I still had in my mind a fresh image of the leg and its wound. I could assist your father in removing what he could not save. It would be no great trouble.

I said, "Course I know what time it is."

"Your husband know you're calling on me?'

"My husband sent me, Hawking. There's a man lying on my table with a crushed leg. Matthew is fixing to remove it, but we need your help. Are you able?"

He stood frowning at me in the dark, swaying on his feet, and after a considerable pause said, "Weeeellll, come on inside and let's see if I am."

Against my better judgment I did follow him inside, where I saw the siege of unmarried life lay upon him and his possessions. Fruit flies danced in the jaundiced light. Dried mud tracks from the bottoms of his boots marked the floorboards. The embers in the fireplace had been dead for some time, and a cloying staleness in the air set my stomach to churning. The business end of the shop was clean as a surgeon's theater, and I wondered if that was not where all his energy went.

The butcher rested the rifle's stock on the floor and opened a cupboard. The bundle he removed had the heft of metal to it. Inside I am sure he had wrapped a hacksaw along with his smaller blades. This he placed in a leather satchel he had left dangling from the back of a chair before mumbling something I could not discern and disappearing down an unlit hall.

Of everything, the absence of light did the least to impede him. I suppose something of his condition could be made of that observation, but I am not in the habit of making much of the things drunken men do in the dark.

When he returned, the butcher wore a leather coat and carried in hand a box of ammunition and a folded object I could only assume was a pair of gloves. Shadows cut ravines into his face. One could see the ghost of the man he had been in his youth, that the years had been kinder to him than he had been to himself. Whatever he was drinking to mask his pain was carving him out faster than he could pour it in.

"Shall we?" he asked, and held out his elbow like he was asking me to dance. That was typical of him, joking when there was no cause for it, and I neither appreciated it in that moment nor did I smile. I waited for him to take back his elbow and extinguish the lamp's flame, and then I followed him out of the kitchen.

Of course I could smell the stink of the horses as I came up the driveway with the butcher, but it was their number that struck me. When I had left to fetch Hawking, two horses were tied at the post.

Now there were three.

Lamplight blazed behind the curtains covering the front windows. Silhouettes burned as black ghosts in the fabric. I counted four. A fist in my gut tightened and tried to pull me back from the house. Hawking had the barrel of his rifle aimed at the ground, but his finger was not on the trigger as he staggered up the drive.

I said, "Hawk, wait a minute."

"What for?" he asked. "I thought you was in a hurry."

"There's a third horse," I said. "There were only two before."

He managed to turn around without losing his balance, though the significance of what I had said was lost on him. He looked at the horses, then looked at me, then back at the horses before giving me a helpless shrug.

"I hate to break it to you," he said, "but I count six."

I said, "Something's wrong. Just please be careful."

Hawking turned back around and approached the house some steps ahead of me, his rifle readied but not raised. Though I had latched it behind me, the door was open, and it allowed the sounds of a commotion out into the front drive. Men's raised voices, your father's low and calm. I could not make out his exact words. A shadow filled the doorway, and as it took substance, I saw it was your father, his bloodied hands held up in surrender.

"You all right, Doc?" the butcher called up.

Your father said nothing.

He looked at me, and time still feels as if it has frozen in that moment. I can close my eyes and watch the explosion of blood and viscera as the lead shells left the muzzle of the blunderbuss and passed through your father's back and out his front.

My refusal to accept what I saw would have proven a useful instrument if I had studied Fate and Time as I have heard tell of other witches doing. But I had not, and in the time it took for me to come to my senses, your father's knees buckled and spilled him onto the porch.

What happened next happened in a matter of seconds, which is what it took for me to start running towards him.

Above your fallen father was the man who had pulled the trigger. The third highwayman, the one my mother meant to warn me of. As clear as I remember watching your father's insides turned out, I remember laying eyes on the culprit. He stood well over six feet tall, and even in his long black coat I could see he had the tapered build of a sailor or a woodsman.

He transferred the blunderbuss to his opposite hand, drawing his revolver and firing two shots at Hawking. The first hit him low in the abdomen, causing him to drop the rifle, with the second hitting him just below the ribs and knocking him into the dirt. The man in the long black coat holstered the revolver and sauntered down the porch steps toward his horse.

Memory is an imperfect record, my dear. I cannot be certain of what I saw that night—whether I saw the man clear as I can see him now. But I would swear to you that before mounting his horse, the man turned and winked at me.

It was then I regained control of my feet. I ran not at the stranger but up the path and towards your father.

Before I could make it any closer, the Mexican came out of the house, carrying the blood-soaked younger man over his left shoulder and holding his revolver in his right hand. He aimed it at me soon as he saw me.

"You follow us," the Mexican said, "I shoot you."

The Mexican reached the horses and hoisted the injured man onto the saddle. I remember now that I heard the hooves of their horses beating as they made their escape behind me.

I took your father into my lap and pulled open his shirt to reveal the churned mess made of the torso I had memorized in darkness and in daylight, the blood bubbling up from so many places, mixing with air to make a pink froth that he coughed up when he tried to speak. And he did try to speak, for while he was dying he was still trying to ensure my safety. He knew what I was trying to do when I scratched the palms of both my hands with my fingernails, drawing blood to the surface and placing them hard and flat against the pumping arteries I knew would kill him in a matter of seconds.

It would have been impossible for your father to feel the ley line opening up between us, even more impossible to feel it draining me of my energy and you, as well. But he knew, because I had told him what a laying on of hands cost me. My body was not my own body. This, he knew. And the fact that the air became charged with the power of my Work, that the wind began to pick up and rustle nearby trees, to rustle my hair, warned him of what I was doing.

Since your father could not tell me to stop with his failing words, he did so with his hands. Those hands that would have taken the butcher's hacksaw and the young man's leg with it, that never trembled even when his mind did so. Hands that lifted me onto his horse and rubbed away at my girlish stubbornness until love shone through. Those hands that would have guided you into the world.

Those hands, cold and bloody, wrapped around my wrists and pulled them away from his chest. I begged him not to, and if I could have enchanted my tears that they would heal him when they landed on him, I would have.

Before he died, he put his hands over my belly. It took him a long time to breathe his last, and we struggled against each other during that time. To me it felt as if only seconds passed, and they did in fact pass. When he passed along with them, I called his name, shook him like he had just gone to sleep and not gone to the Summerland.

But he had. Your father was dead.

6

WHEN I WAS A GIRL, your gran followed my prints in the dust to find I had pulled an old book from the shelf. Though I had never learned Latin, I could recognize its roots in the baser languages I picked up in Texas, and I understood enough. My eyes had found a forbidden spell, one intended to bring the spirit back to a dead body. Your gran had taken me by both shoulders after, looked me right in the eye, and told me I must be very careful when uncovering pages none had touched for so long, for good reason.

As I watched the pall of death settle over your father's body, I thought if I concentrated hard enough, long enough, I could remember the nature and order of the steps necessary to Work that spell. Your father's injuries were beyond what I could repair in a moment, but if I had more time. If I could mend the tears in his flesh, bind his wounds, make him whole again, then I could coax the life back into him. It would not harm you. It would leave me beholden to forces I did not understand, but that would be a small price to pay.

By the time I had decided not to accept what had happened, your father's hands fell away from my belly, and I knew he was dead.

The butcher's coughs halted my thoughts. After that first burst of air, he groaned and commenced to swearing. He had the mouth of a sailor even on his best days, and I am not of a mind to commit any of his words to ink. It would be a simple task to plug the holes in the butcher's belly, and I knew I had to tend to the living before I tended to the dead.

Once I was on my knees in the dirt beside him and had his shirt open, I saw both shots had punched straight through Hawking's body. I hope you never learn to identify a gut shot based on smell. The absence of that stench told me the butcher would live through the night if he held still long enough for me to apply a poultice to his wounds. To make a poultice and return to your father was all I wanted.

I said, "I can fix this."

The butcher tried to sit up, but pain overwhelmed him and he used his heels instead to try to put distance between himself and me. As he did, he asked, "What the hell did you get me into, you damned devil woman?"

Rather than answer him, I left Hawking bleeding and swearing in the drive. I walked past the bloodied table, its chairs strewn aside and the smell of burnt gunpowder in the air. My feet knew the way to the pantry though my mind was no longer with me.

The pantry was undisturbed, and it was from its shelves that I gathered what I needed to seal the butcher's wounds. I placed a palmful of bran into a small clay bowl and added to it a palmful of yarrow seed. These I ground up before bringing the bowl and an armful of bandage back to where he lay. I was careful not to let my tears fall into the bowl as I caught a bit of Hawking's blood in it and then spat to finish my mixing.

"No," he said, "no no no no no, don't touch me."

Before I rolled him to his side, I gave the butcher one of the bandages to bite down on. Then I painted his wounds with the poultice and bound them with cotton and bandage. By the time I was finished, he was pale and sweating, but the blood stopped flowing and the bandages remained clean from gore, which meant my Work had taken.

As I sat back, I thought I saw movement out of the corner of my eye. Your father. It was the wind stirring his hair, perhaps, or a last muscle twinge as his brain followed his body in ceasing to be. In my state, I thought he was trying to get to his feet, so I got to mine, rushing over to him with his name in my throat. It never reached the air. The realization that my mind was playing tricks on me knocked the tears out of my eyes, cold as the night surrounding me. I made no attempt to staunch them. They were all I had, right then.

A clattering of horse hooves and boot spurs came pounding up the path towards us. It was the sheriff and his deputy.

Lieutenant Ness had been clean-shaven and polished. Sheriff Ness, however, wore a thick beard of a lighter pigment than the overgrown brown hair on his head. On any other night I would have thought him here to levy some charge against me. Despite having been a guest in our home more times than I could count, he always looked at me like I was a stain on his shirt, refusing to come up no matter how hard he scrubbed me with his furrowed eyebrows.

I had never seen his deputy before. He was a young black man about my age, a little taller, with kinky hair and winsome features. I would imagine they heard the shots from town. Gunfights were infrequent in De Soto, and when they broke out, the sound could carry for some distance.

Soon as he saw Hawking lying pale and bandaged on the drive, the earth dark with his blood, and your father lying mangled and unmoving across my lap, Sheriff Ness drew his revolver and asked what had happened. I knew he saw a shadow of the situation cast over us, but I cannot recall what I said. What I did was keep my hands on your father as the lawmen took bolder steps, up to the porch and into the house. As they did so, the deputy let go a hushed plea to the lord.

"Yep," said the butcher without opening his eyes.

When I gathered him up again, I found your father's body was losing its warmth. That realization on its own caused me to gasp in a way I reckon frightened the men. I ignored Ness and his deputy and began to stroke your father's hair. My tears had left small red marks where they had fallen on his face, like grease burns from a hot pan. I began again to think of irresponsible things. Of how I could drag your father back across from the other side.

Though I made nothing of it at the time, the sheriff was distraught. He fought against the distress, but his slow, heavy breathing and the choke of salt water in his throat were unmistakable. He looked down at your father's body and me holding on to him, and I had no notion of what was going through his mind.

He crouched down beside me and stared at the mess made of your father's body. His fingertips probed the red marks on your father's face, their redness hot where the blood splatters from the wound that killed him were not.

"Lilian," he said in a voice that would have scared me if either of us were thinking straight, "what happened?"

For whatever reason, I answered true though disordered. "She warned me. She warned me, but I didn't heed her. We had to take his leg, and I couldn't hold him down by myself, so I fetched Hawking, when I came back there were three horses . . ."

Ness's breath shook as he inhaled and returned his revolver to his holster. He pinched the bridge of his nose and blew the breath back out again.

"What are you talking about, Lilian?"

I said nothing.

"Who tried to warn you?"

I said, "My ma," and kept on stroking your father's hair.

"All right," he said, and moved towards the steps as if to follow their trail. "Well, which way did they go?"

I did not answer him.

"Lilian, which way?"

Ness kept talking to me like I was a busted door and he just had to keep working at my lock to open up the way between us. The roaring in my ears began to fade, and in its place I heard accusation. He abandoned the effort after a few seconds and turned his attention to Hawking.

"Roger," he said, "what in the hell happened?"

"What's it look like?" the butcher asked. "I got shot."

"Before that, damn it. Who shot you?"

"I didn't see."

"How many were there? Did you see that?"

"How many what?"

"Three," I said. "There was three of them."

"I thought you said there was two," Ness said.

I shook my head. I had misspoken. Or perhaps the story was coming out stranger than I wanted it to. It was a strange story.

"How many were there?" Ness asked the butcher again.

"How the hell should I know?" the butcher mumbled, his voice a slurry of blood loss and booze.

"You were there!" I said. "Tell him what you saw!"

"Lilian," said the sheriff with an edge in his voice, "let him alone."

"He was here!" I said.

"Yeah," Hawking said. "And look where that got me."

Ness cut me off before I could raise my voice again, asked me where I said they were coming from. So I told him only one of them had anything to say about where they were from. The Mexican had said they were farther west when a band of Comanche fired on them.

"Comanche," Ness said.

"That's what he said," I said.

"Well, I hate to call him a liar, but the Comanche don't stay this far north this time of year. They'd be headed back to Texarkana by now."

Whether he was a liar or not was nothing we were going to sort out that night. That a man who would shoot another man in the back would have lied about the circumstances that led to their arrival in the first place did not seem strange, but even then, something about the youngest of them told me he was no good at either the lying or the shooting. But his lying made me look to be a liar, and it was adding kindling to Ness's doubt. I could see it in his eyes.

"I'll have Deputy Porter send a message out to North Bend and Omaha," the sheriff said. "See if any of that story'll hold water. Meanwhile, I'm going to ride out a bit, see if I can track them."

I said, "Thank you."

"You want help moving him?" he asked.

I said, "No."

"I could send for the pastor. They're going to want to bury him in the morning, you know."

For all I know now, he only meant to offer me hope, to let me know I was not as alone as I felt in that moment. But in that moment, I took it for a threat. All I heard was he did not trust his friend with me in either life or death, and fury began to take grief's place. I said nothing.

The deputy returned then, he and his horse cleaving a silence I had taken for granted. As I had not heard him leave, I made nothing of his coming back. He dismounted and walked back up the drive, told Ness he could find no hoof marks on the trail leading away from the house.

It took both of the men to get the butcher to his feet, and once he was there, the pain of his injuries stole away his breath. Of all the places to take a bullet, the gut has to be the worst. For the first time that night, I almost felt sympathy for the man. Almost, but for the fury. I found my feet and followed them down the steps like I was making sure Hawking would not faint before the deputy got him in the saddle. In addition to assuaging my guilt, it meant I could watch them leave.

Once the lawmen had gone and taken the butcher with them, I could not bring myself to walk back into that house and wait until morning, with the violence still thick in the air and your father dead on the porch.

Even before I began the task of moving your father to the field out back, the thought of going on without him rose up before me, a great fog through which I could not see. This was the house we had built together. The garden, the land it was on, the family we were going to raise, all called for two people. A woman is more capable of raising a child on her own than is a man, and I would not have been the first to do so, but before I met your father I was not a woman. Before I met your father, I was a wild girl loath to let grass grow beneath her feet. Without him, I could not say as I was capable of being a mother. I could raise you, sure, but raising a person and being a mother to them are two different breeds of beast.

My hands were cold when I held you, and the wind come down out of the mountains tugging at my hair was cold, and the trail the three men had taken after gathering their horses and racing into the thickening night was growing cold itself. If I were thinking clear, I would have sought to uncover the bastards' tracks right then. But I was not. I was not thinking at all.

I found no small amount of difficulty in moving your father's body, and I did not want to drag him by his arms, so I went into the bedroom and removed the quilt from the top of the bed, brought it to the porch, and laid it out flat and rolled him onto it the same way I had rolled the butcher to get at his wounds. Once I had him laid upon the quilt, I was able to move him.

You are the first person I have told what I did with your father's body, and why. Death rites are as much a part of our lives as are the union rites, the fertility rites, praising the four winds and the five stages of the moon, greeting the sun in the morning and bidding it farewell in the evening. More than tradition and more than blood, I did not trust myself not to see his body as a liminal component in a ritual I had no business attempting. As an empty vessel needing filling. He did not deserve the fate of Eimhir's beloved, nor had I any intention of meeting her end.

So I went to the stable where the horses stood sleeping and I grabbed a shovel down from the wall and I went back into the yard to dig. Not deep enough to bury a body, but deep enough to bury what the fire would not take. For the last time, I divested him of his clothing. He would not need them where he was going.

Into the pit went kindling and firewood and the quilt and your father's body. When I was satisfied with the sturdiness of the pyre, I went into the garden. There I prepared a bouquet of herbs and flowers to honor and protect his spirit as it made its way to the Otherworld.

I thought of the curiosity I had had about him after he returned me to the roadhouse and our paths diverged. How something had awakened in me when he took my hand the first time. How I hated looking forward to his letters and I hated the relief I felt each time I received one. I thought of all the wasted time in Chicago, how we could have started putting down roots there. Of all the children we did not have because I would have rather chewed carrot seeds than risk raising a wild child in such an orderly city.

The pyre was strong and it burned steady and long, and I stood vigil as the flames caught the shroud I had made of the quilt. After what felt to me an eternity, his body began to burn. The smoke burned my eyes, and tears poured down my cheeks. I watched through the smoke and the tears and I did not flinch when the wind kicked a bit of ash towards me. After the eternity had come and gone and left me there, the pyre collapsed and the fire consumed your father's body.

When there was nothing left for the fire to take, I threw back my head and I screamed. The sky was lightening with dawn's approach and the birds had started calling out to each other and my voice carried like a lone wolf's howl. I screamed as if my pain could bring him back. I screamed without thought. My scream was an instinct, feral refusal to accept what was done, and when I was done, I sat down on the ground beside the pit and I wept. You moved beneath my ribs, your little fists and feet doing what my heart could not—remind me I, at least, was still alive.

All storms end and my own was no different. I was drained, but I still had work to do. My face was darkened with soot, and my tears left clean trails on their way back down to the earth.

Ash and dirt had made a nest of my hair, and my nightgown was stiff with dried blood. I picked up the shovel and began covering the pit with churned earth. This took quite some time, and the effort blistered my hands. I made a small cairn out of stones.

Emptied of tears, I wanted to sleep. Since I could not take your father to bed, I lay down on the dew-damp grass beside the fresh grave and stretched my arm across the dirt as if I were settling against his chest in our own bed.

7

WHEN I AWAKENED, it was with the sun's rays bearing down on my face. The breeze rustled the tall grass, and the moment before I realized why my hands were covered in soot and blood was the last peace I can recall.

As I pushed myself upright, grave dirt clinging to my hair and cheek, the pain in my eyes and throat asserted itself. Reminded me of how I had howled at the starless sky, and how it had remained unmoved by my agony.

All my pain and rage could not convince the Fates to give your father back to me.

I was numb as I found my feet and drifted back into the house. The kitchen was in order, and I had to walk into the dining room to see the first bits of evidence a tumult had occurred. Several chairs were tipped over, and the young man's blood left a sticky silhouette where he had lain awaiting his fate. I inhaled deep and looked down at the floor, hoping one or both of the bandits had stepped in and tracked gore. All I saw was the smeared trail along which I had dragged the quilt bearing your father's body.

So far as I could tell, the man in black had never been here in the first place. I retraced what I thought were his steps the night before, walked as far as your father had before the shot had blown him open. Once there, I narrowed my eyes at the posts providing the porch with a roof. Blood and shot mottled the wood, and I examined its surface before digging into one of the tiny holes to produce a small piece of lead.

I pocketed the lead ball and, memory of the gunshot ringing in my ears, glimpsed the rest of the porch. Your father's blood had dried in an imperfect circle. My arms remembered his dying weight. Footprints large enough to belong to Sheriff Ness brought back his pacing back and forth, choking on his own grief. The butcher's blood would stain the dirt at the head of the drive for some time, but I was not concerned with it. It was your father's blood I could not bear to leave on the porch, echoing his death back at me until I could no longer stand it, and I felt my temper flaring up again as I thought of the mess in the dining room.

While the hearth heated a bucket of water, I poured salt over the bloodstains. When the water was hot and ready, I began to scrub.

Down on my knees and using both of my hands, I welcomed the effort. Not only did it allow me to continue moving in the hopes of outrunning tears, but as I focused on my cleaning I began to believe I could return the blood to your father's body, and he to life. Quick as the thought floated up, I slapped it away.

I must have missed something. I could see clear in my mind the pale face of the wounded young man, hear the accented quality of his English, remember his deference to the Mexican even in the throes of what must have been agony. And I had looked the Mexican in the eye on more than one occasion: when I answered the door, when I stood across the table while he lied about the Comanche and their role in the shooting, when he told me he would shoot me if I followed them. Even if I could not describe the man in black, the wounded man and the Mexican would make a memorable pair.

The trotting of horses and the clattering of an empty cart drawn behind interrupted my work. Before I could empty the bucket to rinse away the lather I had made, Sheriff Ness called my name.

With what was left of my tears lapped up by the ground, I had plenty of room for bile. The sight of the pastor following along in Ness's shadow brought it to boiling.

In our years living in De Soto, I had never had call to converse with the pastor. He was a portly man in his fifties, with thin white hair and watery blue eyes, and neither could I recall his name at the time nor can I do so now. It was unimportant. He was here to collect your father's body, and that was the only reason he spoke to me at all, and he did so as if I were beneath explanation. As far as he was concerned, now that my husband was dead, everything in this house belonged to the territory of Nebraska.

And I, filthy from my work overnight, had no right to be there.

"Lilian," said Ness in greeting, "we're here to collect Matt's body."

I said, "Over mine you will."

"Where is he?"

I did not answer. Ness shared a glance with the pastor, whose face betrayed his disgust, then let himself inside the house. Though I allowed him in, I did not leave him unaccompanied for long. Not once I heard his footsteps, following along the trail of blood I had dragged through the house.

He called my name again, and the pastor followed behind me as I walked slow to join him in the kitchen. He was staring out the window at the garden, and the grave beside it.

"Lilian," Ness said in a low, dangerous voice, "what did you do?"

"He wanted to be buried here," I said. "He told me so. He told me he wanted to be buried here, out back in the garden, so when our grandchildren played under the tree, he could offer them shade. Did you think I was going to let you take him away?"

"Jesus . . ." Ness recoiled as he put together the ash and scent of burned flesh that still hung in the air. It took him some effort to say, "You burned him."

"Sheriff!" said the pastor. "Whatever devilry this woman has done, it has damned Dr. Callahan's soul. She's violated the laws of church and state both, you have to—"

"Let me handle this," Ness said.

The pastor stepped back. My eyes blazed as I watched him cower behind your father's closest friend, who stared down at his boots, shaking his head.

"Lilian," he said, "you're under arrest for unlawful disposal of a body. Are you going to come quietly?"

I took a breath, and when Ness finally looked up from the floor, I punched him in the mouth.

My dear, this was not the smartest thing your momma ever did. Dread soon replaced what little relief throwing the punch had given me, for betrayal darkened Ness's gaze as he wiped the blood from his lip.

"You shouldn't have done that, Lilian," he said.

He was right, of course, but I would not give him the satisfaction of saying so.

To say I did not have a choice would not be true. I could have resisted. I could have run into the fields and thrown out a spell that would allow the sun's rays to cloak me. I could have set the damned house on fire and walked away while the townsfolk rushed to extinguish it. I could have done anything but what I did, but I was tired and your father was dead and somehow, I thought, I would have a better chance of pursuing the three men if I cooperated with Ness.

So I did. I went quietly.

The sheriff and the pastor had come together in a cart, intending to cover your father's body in a shroud and bring it to the cellar beneath the only church in town to await a proper Christian burial. Now they had no body, only a widow with a baby in her belly. Ness locked the shackles around my wrists and helped me climb into the cart.

Banked embers burned beneath my breastbone as the cart clattered down the drive to carry me into town. It was midmorning, and folks who lived and worked along the main street were sweeping their front steps and opening their windows to the fresh summer air, gossiping outside the post office.

Though I had always taken care to look the part of the respectable doctor's wife when I traveled into town, I knew what they thought of me, what they said under their breaths thinking I could not hear them. And in the state I was in that day, shackled and wild-eyed, filthy with blood and earth, they thought their suspicions confirmed. I was dangerous. I was never good enough for your father.

In time we came to the sheriff's office, a modest building with a single wooden chair and a spittoon out on the porch, no curtains on the windows. The pastor and the sheriff exchanged a few low words, the pastor's face pinched and the sheriff placid as ever.

"When word gets out about this," I overheard the pastor say, "folks are going to expect quick dispensation of justice. You know that."

"You worry about God's law," Ness said, "and let me carry out ours."

They parted ways then, the pastor shooting me one last look that said he would have strung me up and done to me what I done to your father's body if he had his say-so. I stared right back at him, at least until the sheriff appeared at the back of the cart and said, "All right, Lilian, let's go."

He helped me down from the cart and passed me off to the jailer, a short man with a bushy mustache and sleepy brown eyes.

The jailer led me inside and locked me up in the third jail cell from the door. With the door shut, I had the distinction of being the only person in custody. The other two cells were made up like mine—a pillow resting atop a folded wool blanket on a wooden bench, a chamber pot and a Bible, and nothing more.

Behind a polished wooden counter were three desks. Two of them were pushed together in the center of the room, the chairs tucked in and the desktops clear of clutter. The third, a rolltop, was flush against the wall opposite the cells. To its right was a door with a placard stating COURTHOUSE. We had not passed the courthouse on the way in, but I anticipated the sheriff would drag me there next.

I sat on the edge of the bed but found I could not abide the roiling in my bones. So I stood. I paced. I scratched the wall with my fingernails, testing its strength. Time ran away from me, and I let it go.

Then came the jingling of the bell over the front door and the heavy thumping of the sheriff's boots against the floor. My hand covered the smear left behind when your father touched me for the last time. I felt you flutter as Ness dragged a chair away from his desk and angled it so I could sit on the bench and look at him direct. I did not sit.

Ness had several years on your father, and the pain in his hip had not subsided in the time since the war. He moved through it, but I saw the stiffness in the way he sat. He leaned forward, fingers knit together, as if we were having ourselves a civil conversation over tea in your father's kitchen.

"How's your jaw?" I asked.

"Lilian," he said, "I'm gonna ask you one more time."

"How many ways you want me to say it?"

"This is the last time I'm gonna ask. You got your story straight now?"

"It ain't a story. It's the truth."

"So let me make sure I got it in my head the way you say it went down. According to you, your ma sent you a message from St. Louis warning you three bandits were headed your way, but there's no evidence of that message anywhere in the house. You and Matt went on about your day, neither of you bringing this message to anyone else's attention, and come nightfall, a Mexican you'd never seen before came to your door, carrying a wounded white man you'd never seen before—"

"Irish," I said.

"What?" he said.

"He was Irish."

"A wounded Irishman you'd never seen before. Matt wanted to amputate, you woke up Roger, the both of you went back to the house, a man in black who neither of you can describe came out, shot Matt in the back, and rode off. That about cover it?"

"He also shot Hawking," I said.

"The man in black."

"Yes. Hawk can tell you."

"Hawk," said Ness, "drinks a fifth of whiskey before noon and doesn't know where he is half the time."

"Then listen to me," I said, imploring as I had not before.

Doubt cast a thick cloud over his face.

"You listen," Ness said. "You say there were three men. Three horses. Now, that's twelve hoofprints and six boot prints. In short, a lot of tracks. I've tracked rustlers. I've tracked bandits across badlands, over solid rock, and I've never lost a trail, Lilian. I have listened to you. I've listened real careful. And I looked up and down the path to your house for the three horses and three men and found two sets of prints. Yours, and Hawking's."

"There were three men," I said.

"We have to exhume the body."

"No!"

"It ain't up to you."

"Just leave him be."

"It ain't up to you!" he said again. "Wasn't up to you in the first place. If you'd have just waited until morning—"

I bared my teeth as I drew a breath to speak, but Ness cut me off.

"Your arraignment is slated for tomorrow morning," he said. "After that, you're to stand trial."

"For what? Burying my husband's body?"

"No," said Ness. "Murder."

Were not for you, my heart may well have stopped then. I felt as if the floor had dropped out from under me. That appeared to be the reaction Ness was expecting, for his expression did not change. He watched me for a moment, then stood, finished with me.

"You'll hang, Lilian. I promise you, you will hang."

Blood-hot tears slid down my face, and I neither stopped nor swiped at them.

In the endless time stretched out after Ness left me to my thoughts, I lived half a dozen other lives. Some of them had me begging for my life, figuring rotting away in prison would be a better fate so long as it meant I could watch you grow up. Some of them ended with me breaking myself out, making my way back to St. Louis, conspiring with your gran and great-aunts and cousins once removed to kill the bastards from a distance. Every one of them, regardless of my own fate, would see you safe with a family who would raise you right. We had no business in Nebraska without your father, and you belonged in St. Louis.

I did not envision avenging your father the way I ended up avenging him. Truth be told, I only wanted to convince the judge it was they, not I, who murdered your father. Since the law insisted on carrying itself out, it might as well punish the right folks. That was where my head was at when the door opened again.

This time, Sheriff Ness wore his weariness like an extra weapon, heavy yet useful. He had his hands on his hips as he strode over to the cell, and he looked at me with a steely cast to his gaze.

"I've spoken to Judge Crewe," he said.

I said nothing. His eyes left mine.

"He's agreed, after you're found guilty—"

"Don't you mean *if?*" I asked, though I knew the answer already.

"You killed your husband, Lilian. Ain't a jury in the land going to believe you didn't."

"I DIDN'T," I said. "I DIDN'T kill my husband!"

"Lilian."

"It was the men, the three I told you about. I would never harm Matthew! You know that!"

He would not meet my eye. I waited for him to, but he kept on staring at the ground.

"Look at me! You know that, Henry. You may not like me, but you know that."

Ness went on, "The judge has agreed, after you're found guilty, to issue a stay of execution until the child is born."

Ness had no sooner given me hope than he had taken it away again. You would be safe, but you would be born in a prison cell. Panic hit me like a bucket of water, and I grabbed hold of the cell bars as the fruitlessness of my appeal became more apparent.

"Hank, please! Please, let me get a letter to my ma; she needs to know what's gone down."

Ness shook his head.

"We should have left you in that cantina," he said, his voice firm but charged with grief.

I knew he hated me, but I could not have imagined what he would say next. He ran his hand down his face, through his beard, and held it over his mouth a moment. Steeling himself to speak in spite of the tears in his eyes. He mumbled through his fingers.

"The judge has agreed to grant me custody of the child once it's free of you."

" . . . what?"

"That child you're carrying is the only thing left of him." He no longer mumbled. He returned his hands to his hips, doubtless so I would not see them shaking. "I won't have it raised in whatever goddamned den you crawled out of."

What wind I had in my sails died then, and I sank back down onto the bench, one hand on my forehead and the other holding on to you. Not despair, not yet, but a kind of desperation began to rattle at the bars.

I was going to spend the rest of the summer, all of autumn, and part of winter in this cell. The men outside would keep me fed and watered like some kind of wild animal, not for my own sake but for yours. They would take you away from me, and they would hang me, and you would grow up thinking Henry Ness was your father. When you began to move your toys without touching them and announce aloud the thoughts of the people around you, when you learned to change the pattern of the wallpaper by enchanting your paintbrush and start fires by Will alone, I could only imagine what they would do to you then.

I did not give one good damn who could hear me on the other side of the wall.

"I have a family. This baby has a family! You have no right to take her away from them, Henry, goddamn you!"

Ness closed his eyes and breathed deeply. Whatever he was about to say, he kept to himself. Then he turned and left the room.

No matter what I did, I would end up back in this cell. My story would end here in Nebraska, at the end of a rope. And yours would begin not with your father, or your kin, but with the lawman who killed your mother.

Silence and I have always had an understanding, and I did not feel threatened by its presence. Truth be told, I preferred silence to the voices of men coming and going, discussing your father's house and your father's body and what they were going to do with me, as if I were not sitting right there listening. I was prepared for a long stretch of silence.

You must be wondering why I did not break myself out of the cell. The jailer had left me with bread and broth and a sneer. That sneer set me to thinking about how I could track down the three bastards who killed your father. So long as they had not crossed a river or, worse, boarded a vessel and headed for distant shores, so long as we were on the same side of the Mississippi River, I would be able to glimpse their location in the bottom of a teacup.

I felt something I had not felt in days. Hope. Hope that I would have justice for your father. Hope that you and I would make it to St. Louis. These two yearnings were at odds with each other, and try as I might, I could not see how one might exist without giving up on the other.

My mother, your gran, always knew what to do. I could pocket a spoon or leave a bit of broth in the bottom of a bowl, use anything I could to reflect a message back to her. If she did not already know what was happening, I could tell her. She and her sisters, my aunts, they would be able to help from afar—if they did not ride out from St. Louis that same night. If that failed, I could focus my fury on the cell's lock, melt the mechanisms. I have heard tell of some witches being able to pass through solid walls, calling on the power of their blood to make their bodies air. Nothing I could do in an instant, but with all this time yawning ahead of me I could sure as hell try. Or I could use a darker shade of magick and hex the jailer into doing as I said. These men were set to kill me, and I was not overrun with sympathy for them.

Amid my musings, the front door creaked open, and a figure stepped into the jail.

It was a short man in a dark overcoat with a hat dipped forward to cover his eyes, though the sun had set hours ago. The man took a few bold steps into the flickering light of the jail, and I cursed out loud when I saw it was Roger Hawking. The bandages I had wrapped around his trunk the night before were where I left them, adding bulk to his otherwise insubstantial trunk. He stood with his hands on his hips a moment, surveying me locked up in the cell.

"Y'know," he said, "gallows bird is not a good look for you."

"Don't you mock me, Butcher."

"Darlin', I ain't mocking you. I'm here to save you. Now hush up so I can think."

"You didn't think you might want to think before you came barging in here?"

He ignored me, going to the jailer's desk to rummage through the drawers.

"What'd you figure?" I asked. "He'd be stupid enough to leave the damn keys in his desk?"

"Hah!" Hawking said, holding up a ring with several brass keys hanging from its thick loop.

I went on, "You going to tell the judge you got into the sauce and didn't know what you were doing?"

"I know what I'm doing," he said, and proceeded to drop the brass ring.

"Wait a minute!"

He ignored me, trying several times to pick up the keys from the floor and dropping them each time. After four tries, I was reaching through the bars to pull them to me when he grabbed them up and shot me a look.

"I know what I'm doing," he said again, and strode towards me.

Through the bars, Hawking smelled like cheap soap and cheaper tobacco, and booze stained his breath as it always did. All that had changed since last night was a large red mark on his hand.

I said, "Would you quit it a minute?"

"We ain't got a minute."

I touched the injured hand, which was holding the jail keys. He stopped and met my gaze.

"They'll come after you," I said. "Ness and his men. Once they catch up to us, they'll hang you right along next to me."

He found the key that fit the lock, fumbled it home, and swung the cell door open.

Now, Hawking was right. I could not sit in a jail cell while those men roamed free. But I had to know that the determination I heard in his voice was not courage on loan from a bottle.

"What are you waiting for?" he asked.

"Tell me why you're doing this."

"Doing what?" he asked, playing innocent.

"*This.* Breaking me out. Risking your own neck."

"Honest," said Hawking, "I don't know what happened to Matt, but I know you didn't kill him. I also know they're going to have me testify, and it won't matter what I say, or how many Bibles I swear on. The jury knows I'm a no-account drunk. They'll paint you out to be a filthy baby-eating witch, and nothing nobody says is going to do a thing to keep them from hanging you. Except for this. Except for breaking you out of here."

"Well," I said after a long pause, "you are a drunk."

That tickled him into laughing and shaking his head. He went on, "I may be a drunk, but I know a giant from a windmill. All I ever seen you do is sprout flowers and patch folks up, including the likes of me, for which, might I add, the distillers of this fine town owe you a considerable debt."

The sad frankness in his eyes ran at odds with his jest, but I did not interrupt him.

"You stay here, they're going to hang you, Lilian. And there ain't enough whiskey in Nebraska to let me sleep with that."

I relented, and in stepping out of the cell became a fugitive.

"You got a plan?" I asked.

"Course I got a plan," he said. "The first part is don't get caught."

"Do I even want to know what the second part is?"

"Here," he said, removing a folded sarape from beneath his overcoat. "Wear this to hide that belly of yours."

I did as I was told.

"Good," said Hawking, rubbing his bruised hand. "That's good. But we really should get gone before the jailer wakes up from his nap."

He held the door open with a flourish, a half-sauced imitation of an upper-class stagecoach driver. Though I shook my head at his foolishness, he did not have to tell me again that it was time to go.

8

THE BUTCHER AND I ARGUED over how long I would have to sneak off into the dark, who Ness would suspect of releasing me, and which direction he would send his men on horseback to search for me. In the end we agreed to meet at the Missouri River crossing fourteen miles to the south, Hawking by cart and I by foot. Once we were certain Ness was not following us, we would cross the river and head south, and we would question people in the towns we came upon if I could not find the bastards by other means.

If I had had my medicine bag with me, I would have been able to construct a charm to dispel suspicion from the butcher, or cast a spell to conceal my footprints or eliminate my scent. As we traveled in pursuit of the three men, I would gather the herbs and stones I needed, but in the meantime all I had at my disposal were my Will and a wild thing's fear of capture.

Our plan, such as it was, hinged on Hawking's ability to gather supplies without drawing attention to himself, and my ability to get out of town without anyone seeing me. It was not arrogance that convinced me the butcher presented a greater danger to our clandestine escape. The man had whiskey on his breath, and I had lived in De Soto long enough to state with certainty that folks on the frontier value routine. It was the only way to survive when everything else lay outside of our control. For Hawking, alcohol was the only thing he could rely on.

Before we parted ways I said, "You stand me up, you're gonna wish you'd left me to rot in that cell."

He said, "Relax, I ain't gonna stand you up."

I crept into the farrier's while the weekend poker game was starting up at the saloon and saddled up your father's horses. Then I led them back to the butchery, where I lashed them to the post outside.

It was in the midst of my work that I heard a whistling and a jangling of spurs. My eyes ripped from the post to spot one of the local merchants swaying out of the saloon a hundred feet or so away. He undid the buttons of his trousers in preparation to mark the side of the saloon, and though I did not doubt he was feeling no pain after the evening's libations, I felt a stab of warning in my gut and ducked behind a horse's flank.

The animal nickered, and the man peered over his shoulder. Our distance was great enough that the darkness and his inebriation provided ample cover, yet I remained unmoving, holding my breath, until he stumbled off again. I looked up and down the street to confirm its emptiness before hurrying down the alleyway leading away from the main street, to the east.

I did not follow a path any sane person would have taken, even in broad daylight. Picking through underbrush and tramping across unkempt fields brought me closer to the river, but it took much longer than I had anticipated.

Over five hours had passed since the butcher and I left each other—and I found it difficult to keep my mind in the present rather than back to the night of your father's death—when I walked through the darkened streets to fetch Hawking, and only the heartless night served as my witness. It would have been easy to let the black memories wash over me as I lay numb, but so is death easy. So was surrendering to Ness's shackles easy. Pursuing the men who killed your father, dragging them back to the Nebraska Territory that they would answer to for their crimes, would not be easy. What is right is not always easy, my dear, but it makes the world a less repugnant place.

I was beginning to doubt I would ever reach the river when I encountered a steep hill and the beginnings of a footpath. I took it back to the main road, and was ready to collapse when I heard hooves behind me.

It was a single rider, a stranger with a lamp in one hand and reins in the other, headed north. I almost dove off the path, but he canted his head and called out to me.

Our kin consider influencing another's life, let alone another's mind, to be dark magick. I did not care. That stranger stood between me and freedom. Between me and justice.

So I asked him what his name was.

He told me his entire name, Thomas Underwood, and once he had done so I thanked him and darted off the path again. My departure startled him, and though he called after me he did not pursue me. Not right away, at least. I used his momentary confusion to crouch in the brush and release a whispered incantation:

Clear water, water clear,

Cleanse Thomas Underwood's mind of my fear

If I had had a white candle, or the appropriate stones, I could have focused my energy and taken less time. As it was, I had only my voice and my Will, and so I repeated the incantation four more times. Then I held my breath and strained to hear the horse and the rider. For a time I could hear only the horse snort and paw the dirt, impatient to get moving again. Seconds passed, the longest seconds of the night, and then the man said, "Huh."

I stayed where I was until I could no longer hear the horse's hooves in the distance, and then I climbed out of the darkness again. With only my filthy shawl around my shoulders, I had grown acclimated to the chill of the night. It was a different sort of breeze that set my flesh to crawling.

Worrying Hawking was waiting and wondering where I was, I kept moving.

Dawn was still several hours off, but the eastern horizon was beginning to lighten, and I was alone at the river crossing. I gathered the hour was three, closing in on four, which I took to mean either Hawking had not yet left town, or he had been taken into custody. We had not discussed what I would do if he did not show up, or if he showed up with a small band of men hell-bent on hanging me. I was beginning to curse myself for having trusted him in the first place, let alone having trusted him with my life and yours, when I heard hooves and cart wheels approaching from the north. I recognized your father's horses at once. In the cart's driver's seat was Hawking, singing an old saloon song.

"Where the hell have you been?" I asked.

He slurred something about making sure we had enough supplies. As your father's horses came to a stop, liquor bottles clinked in the bed of the cart. A cruel toast.

"What," I said, "making sure we don't run out of whiskey before we leave the territory?"

"Or gin," he said as he tried to step down from the cart. Though I warned him not to move, he did not heed me. So I blocked his way down from the driver's seat by anchoring a foot in the wheel's spoke and hoisting myself up.

"Sit down, Hawking, before you break your damned neck." For reasons beyond my comprehension, Hawking started laughing. Before I could ask him what was so funny, he stepped off the front seat and toppled over into the cart, his fall broken by gunnysacks and trunks and rope. All the things we would need for an unseen journey south, fourteen miles of which were covered and a thousand more ahead of us.

I know you must think I did not have you in mind when I set out in pursuit of those bastards. I know you will be angry when you are old enough to think on what happened and why, and I cannot tell you what will happen after I set down this pen. I cannot even tell you I will keep you at my breast until the time comes to pass you off to your gran. But I can tell you I have loved you since before you were born, and I will love you until my bones are dust.

Now that we were moving I did not so much feel peace as a sense of purpose. Having had only my grief for company the past day, to be able to move again felt to me the most natural and welcomed thing in the world.

Riding as fast as I could urge the horses on and still tolerate the jostling, we could not cover more than thirty miles in a day. Keeping to the wagon trails meant we could not cut across the land in hopes of gaining ground, either. If I were not carrying you, I could have taken the one horse and been hot on the bandits' trail, left the butcher behind and pursued them on my own.

That is not a wishing thought. I had not been willing to risk you to save your father, nor was I willing to risk losing you on the road, and so I did not push myself to pursue the men as I would have pursued them were my body my own.

Traveling during the day was unwise, we being still so close to De Soto and our going being so slow. Though the butcher felt the effects of his intemperance in the morning and complained about the day's brightness, he was able to move when I stopped the cart. I watered and set the horses up with their oat bags while he cooked a skillet of eggs and potatoes. I had figured with the two of us we would be able to travel at a steady pace, breaking only for meals and to allow the horses to rest, but I had also figured Hawking would abstain from drinking so as not to make a nuisance of himself. Seeing as that was not the case, I was beginning to believe I would be the one doing all the driving, and it would take us twice as long to catch up with the bastards as I had originally planned.

I returned from the river without cheer, and Hawking looked me over while he pushed the food around the hot pan with a stick. He took a slug from a tin cup and swallowed whatever smart-assed comment he was about to make in favor of returning to the cart. He rummaged around for a moment, then returned carrying an armful of clothes from his wardrobe.

"Go change," he said. "You look like hell."

While the butcher piled food onto plates and began breaking down the cook fire, I took up the armful of articles and disappeared into the trees. I stripped off my bloody gown and washed my body and hair with none but the river for company. The water was cold, but I welcomed its chill after so many days of hot rage and numb denial. I had no mirror to judge whether my appearance was suitable. For the moment, at least, I could button the trousers Hawking had lent me, and though he was not a large man, his shirt would afford my belly room to grow until I found more suitable garments. I wrangled my hair into a braid and pulled my boots back on and stuffed my ruined clothing into an empty gunnysack in the back of the cart.

"There's my favorite witch," said Hawking, surveying me with an approving grin. He attempted a formal bow I have no doubt upset his equilibrium, and presented a plate of what looked to be food. "You ain't never had eggs like these."

"Thanks." And he was right. I waited for him to turn around before removing a piece of bark from my plate. "Mmm," I said, crunching on a forkful. "Earthy."

"Yep," he said, and drained what was left in his cup before belching and returning to the cart for a refill.

Later, as we packed up and returned to the trail, he asked, "How do you know where they're at?"

"One of them stole your rifle," I said. "I've seen where he's keeping it."

"Uh-huh. That all you're saying on the matter?"

I looked at him sidelong, but did not answer. He flicked his eyebrows and I flicked the horses' reins.

Another ten miles passed without a word from either of us, and the evening sun was sinking low in the sky before Hawking asked if I wanted to switch.

"You gotta rest sometime," he said.

"Yeah, I know I do."

"Well, then, gimme here."

"Why?" I asked. "So you can run us into a ditch?"

"All I'm saying," he said, "is it's easier to keep moving than it is to stop and make camp for the night, and quicker besides."

I hated to agree with him, but he was right, and I figured he was used to staying awake most of the night pouring liquor down his throat anyway. Mourning was a heavy cloak, and I confess I was feeling its weight at that moment, particularly since Hawking had stopped trying to make conversation. So long as he was present, I might as well make use of the fact that he was feeling better. Even if I did not need rest, you did.

During the thirty or so days the butcher and I traveled alongside each other, we fell into a routine. It was not comfortable, but it enabled us to keep moving at a steady pace even if, at times, we did not follow the most direct route in pursuit of the three men.

Each time we stopped at a town, we did so under the auspices of being ordinary travelers, weary from the road and expecting nothing from the townspeople. The butcher would go off in pursuit of information and alcohol both while I either procured what I needed from the general store or found a quiet place to Work the spell that kept our prey's trail illuminated.

I would picture the men, the pale young man with the dark eyes and the short yet powerful Mexican capable of carrying him, and introduce a flame to a length of white ribbon. Though I imagined also the man in black, I had not had a clear view of his face and so I could not rely on his image, seared into my mind though it was, to lead me to him. As the ribbon burned I would hold it aloft that the wind would take its ashes, and when the burning was finished, I would be able to see a smoky trail betraying the path they had taken. Sometimes the ritual would finish by the time Hawking returned from the nearest tavern. Many times it would not. He never interrupted me, but only packed up the cart and saw to the horses while I completed my Work. Then we would confer, and we would continue on again.

One day, as we were traveling along a long stretch of empty road, the butcher turned to me and asked how old I was when I knew I was a witch.

I asked him, "How old were you when you knew you were a drunk?"

He laughed and shook his head and kept right on drinking. That was, I suppose, the best answer I could hope to receive for some time. But drunks are doomed to repeat the past for not keeping hold of their memories, and whether he forgot having asked me the first time or whether he asked me again thinking he would produce a different outcome, he did ask me again.

We rode on for a time and then I told him, "I was born a witch. Wasn't until I commenced to converse with others my own age that I knew what it meant."

"Was your momma a witch too?"

"Still is," I said.

"What about your daddy?"

"Never knew my daddy."

"Your momma cook you up in a cauldron or what?"

"I didn't say I didn't have a daddy. I said I never knew him."

"Shit," he said, and turned to face me more fully. "Where were you born?"

"Missouri."

"Oh," he said, and relaxed. "I ain't ever been to Missouri."

"Wouldn't matter if you had. You ain't my ma's type."

"What's her type, then?"

I shrugged and said, "Seems to me she likes men that don't stick around."

This struck Hawking as so humorous that his laughter brought on a coughing fit. I walloped him on the back to help clear the tar from his lungs and told him it served him right.

He let the matter lie for a few days afterwards, a rainy spell and our concern for the trail washing us away keeping us from conversation. But when the sun returned, so did Hawking's curiosity.

"Y'all do use cauldrons, though, don't you?"

"What?" I said, for the question had come out of nowhere and startled me. "No, we don't use cauldrons. Well, none of my kin do, at any rate."

"How many of there are you?"

"Not as many as there used to be. Too many for the church's liking."

"Which church?"

I shrugged and said, "Any of 'em. Ma and my aunts used to tell us girls stories when we were growing up, how our ancestors left Scotland on account of the witch hunters. We had to behave as if we were no different than anyone else, or the hunters would get us."

He considered this in silence for a time. Finally he said, "I ain't been a drunk my whole life."

"I figured not," I said.

He took another pull off his flask.

"So what all can you do," he asked, "besides heal folks and give me a hard time?"

I shrugged. Truth was I could do anything I put my mind to, so long as I devoted my time and attention to mastering its application, and I told him so. As a young girl I could cause objects to levitate, and move from one end of the house to the other without walking or using doors. Life among mundane folks had replaced my changefulness with caution.

I lost track of all of Hawking's questions, for he would ask me on and off about many of the truths I have already recorded for you. Some of the questions he asked were not ones I would have thought to ask, such as whether there are such things as man witches (to use his words) or if witches come from any-place other than the British Isles. A few of them I refused to answer, such as whether folks from outside of magickal families could learn magick, or whether we could read minds.

On a particular occasion, I was the one asking after his origins.

He answered, "Hell . . . I been in De Soto about four years now, maybe five. What year is it?"

"It's 1859," I said.

"Damn," he said. "You sure?"

After three weeks of keeping good pace with the bandits, we were stopped outside Memphis, Tennessee, when the ribbon burned and turned to ash but did not reveal a path. I watched the wind carry the last of it away, then lit another, certain I had allowed my thoughts to stray or some distant noise to distract me. But the second ribbon yielded no more fruitful results. I was preparing to light a third when the butcher returned, and I swore, throwing the matches into the cart and staring to the east.

"The hell's the matter with you?" Hawking asked as he loaded a crate of gallon jugs into the back.

"I lost 'em," I said.

"How'd you do that?"

"They must've crossed the river."

"That'll do it, eh?"

"That'll do it," I said.

"Well, shit," he said. "Guess we better cross the damned river."

On the ferryboat carrying us across the Mississippi River, we saw the leaves changing to orange and yellow on the trees. Hawking and I questioned the ferryman about the bandits, and he seemed unimpressed until I mentioned one of the men was Mexican.

"Oh, yes," he said after that moment of uncertainty, "I seen 'em prolly two weeks back."

"How many were they?" I asked.

"Just him and his buddy."

"What'd his buddy look like?"

"Oh, let's see here . . . real dark eyes, kinda skinny. Didn't do much walking around."

On the other side of the river I lit another ribbon, this time focusing not on the wind but on my memory of the young man's face. It did not work, and I did not bother swearing.

"Now what's wrong?" Hawking asked.

"It ain't working," I said. "I can't light up their path anymore."

"Why's that?"

"I've no idea. Maybe the current washed it away. I'll have to pick it up again somewhere else."

"We'll find 'em," Hawking said. "If the ferryman remembers them, we've gotta be going the right way."

"I suppose you're right," I said.

We decided to head south, figuring if no one in Senatobia, Mississippi, a day's ride away, had seen them, we could swing east and try our luck there. But we did not have to swing east. Hawking's time in the taverns was not solely for his benefit, it seemed.

"I," he said in triumph, "have been a drunk longer than you've been burning ribbons, and those two sons of bitches passed through here two weeks ago."

"So they're headed south," I said.

"It would appear so."

It appeared so in Pope, Mississippi, as well as Grenada, Mississippi, which is when I next proposed I attempt to light their trail again. That made the butcher laugh. "You don't need no magic ribbon to see where those two are going," he said, taking a deep breath.

"Oh, really," I said.

"Put yourself in their boots a minute. You're wanted men, one of you is a filthy Irishman and the other one's from Mexico, and the law's sniffing after you. Are you gonna go east, where you can't break wind uptown without folks hearing about it downtown, or are you gonna go to the one place where odds are a one-legged dimwit and a Mexican with an itchy trigger finger are going to be the most well-behaved people in the room?"

"And where would that be?"

"The Crescent City, darlin'," he said. "New Orleans."

We veered southwest until we found the Mississippi River again, somewhere outside of Vicksburg, where the air began to turn to soup. Outside Natchez we spied a sign pointing travelers towards the steamboat landing in the distance and argued for a spell as to whether we would continue as we were or if we ought to sell the horses and the cart.

In the end, logic and I won. We could not be certain what would happen in New Orleans, and if we found the three men, we would need the supplies to bind them and the cart to transport them. So we continued on without further incident, until the night we prepared to conquer the last thirty miles into the city of New Orleans.

I lay down in the back of the cart, as was becoming usual, and used a sack of oats to support my knee, as lying on my side was the most comfortable position. If I were back at the roadhouse, my mother and my aunts and my cousins would inundate me with advice, mix up potions and balms, and all but tuck me in at night.

As the sun rose over the swampland, I entered the hazy realm between dreams and wakefulness, the place where visions wait. This morning, one found me.

A bear behind steel bars, pacing the length of its cage, sniffing at the ground. It stopped and lumbered towards me, stood on its hind legs with a curious turn of its head. We stood watching each other until, without warning, it let out a roar that chilled my blood. It was not meant for me. It was meant for what was behind me. I jumped back from the cage and awakened with a jolt.

"Jesus!" said Hawking as I sat upright and held my hand over my belly, where you were restless and kicking. He turned around in the driver's seat and asked, "You all right back there?"

"Your cooking is beginning to affect my dreams," I said, to the butcher's amusement. "Where are we?"

"Welcome to the iniquity capital of the United States," he said.

9

NEW ORLEANS FELT to me as if I had stepped off the boat to find myself in another country, with only a madman to guide me along. Though he was quite deep in his cups after riding all night, he would not yield the reins to me.

"We ain't in the North anymore," he said. "You need to act right."

I said, "Excuse me?"

"Nobody with half a brain in his skull is going to take you for a man, even if you are wearing pants. I'm just trying to keep you out of trouble."

"What in the hell are you talking about, Hawk?"

"Just watch your mouth, is all I'm saying."

I snorted, as a snort was as close to responding without acquiescing as I could come. Before I could ask the butcher what made him such an expert on local culture, he said, "So our first order of business ought to be finding a room for the next couple nights. Then we can start asking around the saloons, see if anyone's seen these lowlifes."

"Saloons," I said. "Might've figured. Only evidence you're gonna find there is the proof on the front of a damned whiskey bottle."

"You got a better idea?"

"Not an idea so much as a vision," I said. "I saw something last night, in my dream, as we were passing through the swamp."

"Bayou," he said.

"A what?"

"Bayou," he said again in a drawl.

"What the hell is a bayou?"

"A swamp," he said.

"Whatever you want to call it, I saw something in my dream."

"You seen where my rifle's at?"

"No. Something else."

"So you have been dreaming about me again."

"Just drive the damn cart."

Ours was among the only carts moving along Tulane Avenue, which I would later learn is one of the city's main streets. I noticed rails embedded in the stonework but made nothing of it until I heard the clopping of other horses' hooves. That was when I gasped.

"What's got into you?" Hawking asked.

The horses were pulling neither a cart nor a stagecoach but rather a car, not unlike what one might find pulled along by a steam engine. This car, for lack of a better word, was made of wood and painted red, with white lettering. People sat on benches inside, if they did not stand and hold fast to poles fastened to the floor and the roof for such a purpose.

"I've never seen such a contraption before," I said.

"What? You never seen a horsecar?"

I shook my head.

"Damn," he said, and started laughing. "Girl, you need to get out more."

"I get out plenty."

"Dancing bare-assed underneath a full moon don't count, you know."

"I will push you off this cart," I said.

He just laughed and urged the horses on, granting me a fuller opportunity to study the horsecar and its occupants.

Out of the din created by strolling women and shouting youths, ringing bicycle bells, and music drifting down alleyways from unseen courtyards, I heard a different voice. Separate from the others, above them. A clear, brilliant tenor, calling out rather than singing.

The next horsecar was filled. I took a second blinking look to assure myself of what I had seen. It was not a passenger car at all, but rather a small steel cage. Inside the cage was a hulking mound of thick brown fur, the smell of hay and urine preceding it, unsupervised children and unoccupied adults following after for a longer look.

"Stop the horses," I said, and repeated myself loud when Hawking looked at me in confusion.

"All right," he said, and frowned deeper before urging the horses to pause a moment.

He turned to watch not the bear, but me as I gathered up the trouser fabric as I would have a skirt and hurried to the back of the cart.

That clear voice began to articulate itself into words, and I looked ahead to find the source of the announcement. Hawking stayed where he was, reins held still in his hands, uncertain as to what had gotten into me.

"That's right, folks!" said the fellow, who was hanging off the back of the next car. "All the way from the Golden State, killer of man, livestock, and children alike, the fearsome grizzly bear! Don't get too close! She may seem harmless now, but tonight, and tonight only, a single shiny dime will earn you entrance to the mother of all fights! She's killed hunting dogs, she's killed mountain lions . . . why, she's even killed a full-grown bull, can you imagine? Tonight, she takes on a pack of wolves, ladies and gentlemen, the most dangerous and destructive of all nature's creations, right here in New Orleans! Stop by Dauphine Street between San Louie and Conti Streets. The event will begin at nine o'clock sharp!"

His voice continued to carry even after his car had passed us by. I was breathing fast, my jaws aching, when Hawking reached back and clamped a hand on my shoulder.

"Whoa," he said, and held up his empty palms when I whipped back around. "Calm down, it's me."

"Bear," I said. "You heard what he said, right?"

"I think they heard him in Mexico."

"There was a bear in my vision last night, Hawking."

We resolved to find lodgings with a view of the fight.

I took note of the names of the streets we traversed and where they were in relation to other destinations. If I were alone, I would have had to stop and ask for directions. My driver, who I could not believe was still conscious after all he had had to imbibe, let alone that he was still upright and coherent, did not stop once.

"I thought you were from New York," I said.

"What?" Hawking said.

"Do you know where we're going?"

"You seen one city, you pretty much seen 'em all."

Not in the mood to argue with him, I decided to let the matter rest for now. Blood had its way of outing, after all, and we had a long trip back to the Nebraska Territory ahead of us. At least, that was what I thought, and what I think Hawking thought, as we climbed down from the cart and paid the stabler and went into the hotel.

"Lemme make sure I'm understanding you," Hawking said, holding the door open for me. "A bear spoke to you in a dream and told you to stay at this snobby hotel?"

"Not in so many words," I said.

"And she says I ain't got a plan."

Though I would not give him the satisfaction of telling him so, the moment we stepped inside I knew Hawking had a point. It was a far grander place than I had ever been in before, with parquet floors in the entryway and corridors and what appeared to be marble in the lobby. I felt every bit the uncivilized hag those who would string me up would have named me, and Hawking appeared to have been inebriated for a week straight. He had not shaved, and neither of us had bathed in some time.

The courtyard was strange, filled with plants whose leaves were like big green feathers, their trunks like an insect's carapace. Vibrant flowers with names I could not recall, having never encountered them before, filled pots and boxes. And then there was the matter of the pool.

"Why've they water in the center of the courtyard?" I asked in a low voice as we made our way along the breezeway.

The water in question filled a depression that appeared from our vantage point to be at least six feet deep and shaped like a rectangle. Its color was a foul green, but that had not been enough to stop a family of five from donning ankle-length gowns and floating about in it.

Hawking said, "That's called a bathing pool, dear."

I managed not to hit him until we were well clear of public view, with the door shut behind us and locked against intrusion. Though we had little to carry, neither did the room afford us much in the way of space. The proprietor had presumed us married and installed us in a room with a single bed and a single bath. That we did not have to share this bath with the rest of the floor was enough to give me pause, but then I realized we would not have to pump water from a well to fill the tub either.

At the window overlooking the street, I began to feel the grime of the road in my hair and under my fingernails. Hawking continued to complain about my lack of any plan, calling me "damned devil woman" and a slew of other vulgarities.

The tub did not have any water in it. There were two strange knobs and nothing to draw up the water. I had to swallow my pride and ask Hawking how to use it.

"Maybe the bear will tell you," said Hawking, plopping on the bed.

I slammed the bathroom door to mute his laughter.

After fiddling with the knobs for a time, a scalding hot torrent of water flowed into the tub. When I came out over an hour later, my digits gone to raisins and the water so cold that my skin pimpled as the air met it, Hawking was facedown on the bed, breathing heavy but not snoring. I took his hat from where it half covered his face, then pulled off his boots and unfolded the blanket at the end of the bed. He did not stir as I draped it over him.

I intended to pull the curtains closed when I walked over to the balcony doors, their glass inlays allowing the late-afternoon sunlight into the room, but I had never stayed in a hotel room before, let alone one with a balcony. So I let myself out, stepping around the iron table and its uninviting chairs to rest my hands atop the rail. The temperature high as it was, I had taken to rolling up the cuffs of the oversize shirt until they reached my elbows. Likewise, I rolled up a handkerchief and used it to hold my hair off my neck. A slight breeze blew down the street and offered some relief to those of us out of doors. I heard a low noise I could not identify in the street below.

A large cage, at least eight feet tall and three times that length, stood in the middle of Dauphine Street. While the horses were nowhere to be seen nor the wolves the crier spoke of, the cage was not empty. I heard the noise again.

It was the bear. She was whining, a low, pained noise.

Were Hawking awake I suppose he would have asked me what I was doing and tried to stop me. But he was not, and so I slipped out of the room unaccosted.

In the street, men stood outside public houses with their shirts unbuttoned to reveal their chests, smoking cigarettes and laughing loudly. This was a different country, and I did not intend to remain here long enough to learn the customs or the laws.

Without a breeze, the smell of the bear's litter stung my eyes. I came to just outside arm's reach of the cage, and the beast stirred and pricked its ears. I saw no signs of injury, and when she turned her head towards me, I sensed neither hunger nor anger. She would not try to attack me through the bars.

This is a foolish act I undertook, and yet I undertook it anyway. I reached between the bars to splay my fingers across her flank, to read the energy of her bones and muscles. I began to wonder what would happen if I were to undo the cage latch. If the bear would find its way home peacefully, or if it would leave mangled corpses and missing children in its wake.

It was not the threat of catastrophe that convinced me to leave the cage locked and step away. It was necessity. Without the cage, there would be no spectacle, and it was the spectacle Hawking and I were counting on to draw the highwaymen out of hiding.

A low groan left the bear's chest, a note of understanding or forgiveness in its tone. Perhaps you think your mother crazy, reading this, but I know the bear would not have harmed me even if I had unlocked its door. It lifted its snout once, then lowered its head again. I took it as a missive to go. So I did.

I returned to the room to find Hawking had not stirred, which was just as well. While I waited for him to resurface, I lay down atop the bed, as far from his corpse-like stillness as I could. I hummed at first, finding my voice somewhat dusty after so long on the road. But I did find it, and though I would have never sung for my own sake, I sang for yours. Judging by the movement I felt beneath my ribs and the palm of my hand, it was not a wasted effort.

In time the daylight faded and the sky lost its color and the inkiness of night overcame it. Music belonging to a genre I had never heard before drifted over the rooftops, and the crowd began to gather. Hawking returned to consciousness with a deep breath.

"What time is it?" he asked.

"Almost time for the show to start," I said.

He rolled to his feet without further complaint and went into the bathroom to change his clothes and wash his mouth. I protested when he did the former without shutting the door, and when he reminded me it was nothing I had never seen before, I hid my face beneath one of the pillows.

Hawking's idea of tidying up involved running the water in the sink for perhaps two minutes. I did not remove the pillow from my face until I heard him secure the clasps on his suspenders, and when I did, I did so in time to catch him gargling, a bottle of whiskey in hand.

"Charming," I said as he spat into the sink.

He said, "Ain't I?" And punctuated the question with a long pull from the bottle.

"Come on, it's nearly nine o'clock."

"I'm comin', I'm comin'."

We went out onto the balcony, Hawking pocketing the room key and pushing his feet into his boots as he left. The entire street below was ablaze, oil lanterns set up along the sides of buildings if they did not have their own posts from which to hang. Other tenants had lit candles atop their balcony tables to see their companions better.

The closer we came to the cage, the more the faces of the individuals composing the crowd blended together, their features indiscernible in the low light. Hawking and I stood next to each other in silence, and though he took another pull from his bottle, the sloshing of the liquid seemed to me as much an admission of uncertainty as his voice would have.

"I can't see anyone from up here," I said.

"Neither can I."

A swell of voices heralded the arrival of the car containing the wolves. The effort of releasing the animals into the cage without allowing one side or the other to escape required co-ordination on the handlers' part, but the way the young men walked atop the cage and pulled partitions up and lowered them again was as fine a display as I imagine a ballet performance would have been.

When the wolves were free to move from one cage to the next, the handlers scrambled away from the cage, and the crowd began to lose its composure. The wolves, six altogether, began to fan out in front of the bear, their hackles raised and their lips curled back into snarls I saw even from my place on the balcony, the lamplight illuminating their teeth and the soulless black of their eyes.

The bear was sat back on its haunches, facing the approaching wolves but doing nothing to meet them in battle. It loosed another low moan and the wolves circled it, nipping at it as if to judge its health before striking.

With the first snap of animal jaws came another swell of cheering. Still the bear did not attack the wolves. It leaned back into itself and bellowed. Though the three wolves still before it lowered their ears and sank lower onto their front paws, it was clear they would run if they had the opportunity. Behind the bear, the other three wolves paced back and forth, making high-pitched harrying noises and snapping at the bear's legs and back.

From where we stood, I judged the crowd rapt but could make out nothing of the individuals within it. They were a single mass of hats and hollering. If any of the three we sought stood among them, I could not sieve them out.

So I quit the balcony and hurried through the room. Though I said nothing to warn him of my intention, Hawking followed me down to the street below.

Our view of the cage diminished once our feet touched Dauphine Street, as did our view of the crowd. Faces were easier to glimpse up close, but they were so packed together and focused on their desire for a fight, I found identifying anyone impossible. I grabbed hold of Hawking's shoulder so I would not lose him in the crowd, and aside from a quick uncertain glance back at me, he did not react.

A commotion began to roll over the crowd, response to activity at the far end of the cage I could not see. With the men wearing hats and the women wearing capes, I could not see much of anything at all. The hand that was not on Hawking's shoulder I kept around you.

As we drew closer I heard the bear's whining, louder and frantic. I heard the crier's voice, but so soon as he began to speak, his words disappeared beneath the wave of booing and hurled insults. A break in the crowd allowed Hawking and I to the front, and a silence rolled over those who saw what I saw.

I cannot recall if the bear began to whine again, or if in writing this I am imagining her desperation.

The handlers had her cub.

It was my voice joining the crowd's this time, though theirs was lifted in exhilaration and mine in fury. I shouted, "No!" at the handlers, as if my protest would make any difference. They lassoed the cub into the cage, then released it. The wolves reacted with a quickness their appearance belied, all six responding as one to surround the cub.

That was what it took to rouse the bear. She reared up on her hind legs, standing almost too tall for the cage, then swiped at the first among the wolves to turn its back on her. It yelped as her claws destroyed its hind leg and hurled the wolf against the far side of the cage, its blood splashing the cobblestone beneath them. It did not rise again. Her bulk suggested she ought to lumber, but the bear moved faster than the wolves to try to put herself between the attackers and her cub.

By then Hawking had taken firm grip of my upper arm to keep me from acting without thinking, but I could not have told him whether I was more compelled by the horror before me or my search for the men who had murdered your father.

To say this was an event that would occur only in a place like New Orleans affords the rest of the country more than its due. This is a practice only monsters would think to profit from, and yet these monsters were human. The crier and the crowd and the whole of the city itself. Civilization and savagery are quite capable of living side by side. Never let anyone tell you otherwise. These same folks watching man's manipulation of nature would have cheered just as loud were they witnessing a hanging.

As the bear returned to all fours and moved to reproach the two wolves surrounding her baby, the three behind her leaped. One of them landed high on her back, sinking its fangs into her neck, while the other two began to chomp at her hind legs. The bear roared again, fury overtaking her grief, and threw herself at the cage bars closest to the cub. Bones crunched and another of the wolves yipped, losing its hold on the bear's leg and crumpling to the ground. She clamped her teeth into the fallen wolf's throat, shook her head once, twice, a third time, then batted it away as if it were a minor nuisance she could no longer attend to.

Again, she threw herself at the bars. And again. And again, until the steel bars began to crack in their grids.

Not until the bars cried out in distress did the crowd do the same. Those on the far side of the cage grabbed hold of their loved ones and fled, some of them screaming, most of them not looking back.

A few more blows from the bear and the bars snapped open, jagged pieces of steel flying into the street with the un-injured wolves attempting to do the same. The biggest of the wolves caught the bear's claws, and when she dispatched the animal and swung again, she seemed to do so blind. An au-dience member who was too close to the cage when it broke clamped his hand over the great gash left behind on his chest and continued running. Those wolves who still had the ability to do so joined the crowd in fleeing down the street.

As the northern end of the street emptied, a distant figure caught my attention, not because of anything it was doing, but because it was standing still.

"Hawk," I said, "look!"

It was the Mexican.

"Who's that with him?" Hawking asked.

I did not know, and moving closer did not help me identify his companion. Though she was about as tall as he, she had a willowy form and long blond hair where he had wiry limbs and brown skin. From a distance I could only hazard a guess as to her age, but I could make out neither hips nor breasts. What I could make out were boots with heels so high as to be obscene, black stockings, and a skirt hem that barely covered what little she had to show. Her arms were bare, her dress more of a shift.

We were perhaps fifty feet from the cage when gunshots began erupting behind us. I do not know whether Hawk threw me down or whether I went to my knees on my own, but either way I broke my fall with one hand and kept the other wrapped around you. When the firing ceased and all that echoed in the air was the ghost of violence, he was shielding me with his body.

My dear, you will find that just as your gift allows you to heal, it also means you will feel the pain of others. As did the bear and her cub, so did I feel their last moment of pain and fear and anguish.

"Son of a bitch," Hawking said as we regained our feet.

The Mexican was gone, and the girl along with him.

It was my turn to swear.

"It's all right," Hawking said with a sigh. "I know where they're going."

10

I CANNOT TELL YOU the moment I began to think of Roger Hawking not as an imposed companion but as one I trusted, as a friend. I can tell you I knew nothing of his history when we arrived in New Orleans, other than what I had heard murmured in De Soto. Had he told me the truth, I would not have judged him. Even now, I do not judge him. I know nothing of what it is to be a husband, or a father, or a drunk.

After the madness in the street had subsided, he and I set off into the night together. In spite of my bare feet and poor preparation, I found the night air tolerable, and I wanted for neither shoes nor shawl. What I wanted was an explanation. I asked Hawking where we were going.

A strange expression came over his face, as if he would answer true were it not for the presence of an impediment. Spells exist that are capable of stopping a person's throat, if not their tongue, from betraying a particular truth. He was under no such spell. He did not want to name the place.

I kept to his side and watched the alleyways and side streets, as Hawking was either oblivious to his surroundings or unconcerned with what might be lurking in the darkness.

Once we arrived at the canal, we passed by saloons lit by lanterns and match strikes, and doorways crowded with bodies in various forms of congress. Someone hiding in the shadows whistled sharp and lascivious at us. I assumed he was whistling at me. As I was wearing Hawking's clothing, he very well could have been whistling at either of us. New Orleans, as I have written, is a lawless place.

We came at last to a building that appeared, in its size and grandeur, to be the only house on the street. To call it a house would imply it was a home. This was not a residence, terraced like many of the others in the neighborhood, nor was it strictly a place of business. It was more akin to a mansion than anything else, a wide yet shallow bit of construction meant to look impressive from a distance. Beautiful though it was, it had an ugly aura.

It was at the end of the street that we, or rather Hawking, hesitated. I did not realize he had done so until I found myself several steps ahead of him. Hawking stared at the front steps, and I shall never forget how distant he was.

I pressed on, Hawking trailing me up the steps to the open front door. We followed the entrance hall to find ourselves in a mezzanine. It was grander than any hotel I could have possibly imagined, and everything from the flooring, to the decor, to the furniture seemed to have come out of a storybook.

This neighborhood was, in fact, called Storyville. I did not know that at the time. We were in the city's red-light district.

As I was gaping at our surroundings, I almost missed the approach of the establishment's procuress. Then the clicking of her kitten heels reached my ears. I looked over to see a woman who appeared as lavish and plush as the place itself, wearing a blue silk evening gown with a neckline so deep its stitching just barely contained her ample breasts. She wore her kinky black hair parted down the center and rolled into two buns at the back of her head, which she covered with a frill and nothing more.

When she saw me, her painted lips pulled into a smile. Her eyes traveled up and down my form, and I planted my hands on my hips in what I meant to be a fighter's stance. She did not touch me. Instead she circled the two of us, making a pensive noise as she passed behind us, and when she came around again, she was still smiling.

"Well, the clothes won't do, but the merchandise might," she said in a thick Cajun accent.

"Excuse me?" I said.

"You," she said, "you have an exotic beauty many a man would pay extra to pass a good time with."

"She ain't for sale," said Hawking.

"Oh, my hand, I was just playing."

With a last long look at me, the madame sucked on an eyetooth and crossed her arms over her chest before granting Hawking her full attention. She gave him the same up-and-down she had given me, this one full of derision.

"If you come here for a girl," she said, "I ask you bathe before you lie with her. They women, not animals."

She gave him more thorough consideration this time, her eyes lingering on his face, and she made that same thoughtful noise as before, this time with more depth to it.

"Are we old friends?" she asked Hawking.

Hawking said, "No."

"Well, if we not old friends, and you don't want new friends, what you want?"

"We're looking for a girl we saw earlier," I said. "About my height, skinny as a rail, yellow hair?"

"Ah," said the madame, "you're in luck. Come. I show you to her room."

While the curtains had kept from the world the activities behind them, the doors had a tougher task before them. Hawking and I followed the madame up a winding staircase, and as we passed by several closed doors, I heard murmurs and cries. We passed through what seemed to me a pantry or another form of closet, and finally came to a door, slightly ajar and lit by lamplight.

The madame rapped on the door with her fighter's knuckles and eased the door open.

Inside, the floor was covered from one wall to the next in pink carpet, its walls papered with a design of delicate flowers. Sex and perfume both hung heavy in the air, and something else, something cloying and rotten. The girl to whom the room belonged was seated by the window, wringing out a washcloth she had been using on herself a moment earlier. When we entered, she grabbed a robe and covered herself almost in one motion, her blue eyes wide as a woodland animal's.

Those wide eyes met those of the procuress and made a wordless exchange.

"Oui, Madame Lavoie."

Once Madame Lavoie had gone and shut the door behind her, I said, "Now look, we ain't here to fool around. We got some questions for you, that's all."

"Y'all gonna pay me?" the girl asked.

"Of course," I said.

The girl cinched the robe's belt around her waist and draped the washcloth over the edge of the basin, eyeing me with lingering suspicion and Hawking with more open curiosity. Her childlike appearance from a distance did not diminish altogether now that we were closer, but her coltish limbs and flat trunk made me wonder if she had held aspirations of being a dancer one day.

"What do you want me for?" she asked, a toughness in her voice I imagine she had heard the other girls use and was trying out for the first time.

"We just need to ask you some questions," Hawking said, "and then we'll be out of your hair."

She nodded, her eyes flitting back and forth between us without seeming to blink.

"It's all right," I said. "We need information about the man you were with at the animal fight earlier this evening. What's his name, and who was he with?"

"What man?" she asked.

I crossed my arms over my chest, considering the consequences of what I was about to do. My eyes searched the room, quick, before landing on a pitcher of water beside some drinking glasses. I picked up a glass and filled it halfway with water, then danced my fingertips over it. Though I did not look at Hawking, I could feel his eyes on me.

"I wasn't at the fight tonight," the girl said.

"Did you know there was a fight?" Hawking asked.

She hesitated before saying, "No."

I turned back to her and held out the glass.

"You look parched," I said. "Drink some water, sit down, relax. This doesn't have to be so stressful."

She eyed me with some suspicion, but took a sip of water all the same. Then she set the glass down on the windowsill and sat down on the chair she had abandoned. She uncrossed her arms, her limbs loose and splayed.

"The man you were with at the fight," I said. "What was his name?"

"Lorenzo," said the girl without hesitation.

"You get his full name?"

"The other fellas called him de la Cruz."

"You saw the men he was with?" I asked.

"Yes," the girl said.

"What were their names?"

"Kelly, I think, was the other one. His leg . . ."

She shuddered and could not finish her sentence for the revulsion it brought up. Hawking looked over at me with one brow quirked, but he did not interrupt me or ask any questions of his own. He just leaned back against the doorjamb and watched.

"It's all right," I said. "I can imagine the state he was in. Who else was with them?"

"I don't know his name."

"Tell me what he looked like."

"Tall. Handsome. Blue eyes, blond hair. Wore all black. He . . . he did things."

"What things?"

"I can't," said the girl.

"Please," I said, "tell me what he did."

"They hurt themselves, because of him."

"The girls? How? How did he make them hurt themselves?"

She was becoming upset, but because of the spell I had Worked on her, she could not outright refuse to answer my questions. Hawking picked up on this, and he spoke up.

"Can you show us what he did to them?"

The girl nodded, and Hawking stepped away from the doorjamb. Without another word, we followed the young woman out of the room.

She took us back the way we had come, but rather than passing through the cupboard again, she opened a door that led into a narrow corridor. Even with gas lamps installed every few feet, the corridor was dark and smelled of disuse. It gave way to a stairwell, which we descended until we came to a room at the back of the mansion. She did not knock before she opened the door, allowing us inside. A single cot stood among crates and other items wrapped up for storage.

On that cot lay a girl even younger than the one to whom we were speaking. Fifteen, at best. The girl's face was wrapped in bandages, the wounds seeping brownish red through the once-white linen.

I thought of who she might have been, before she met Madame Lavoie. Of whether it could have been me there, had I stayed lost in Texas. Of whether this might be you one day, with no mother or father.

My sadness and compassion returned to fury. This girl did nothing to deserve her fate. The man in black forced it upon her.

"Jesus Christ," said Hawking.

The girl on the pallet did not move.

"What's her name?" I asked our guide, though I did not know her name, either.

"Grace," said our guide.

"Grace," I said, "who did this to you?"

She did not respond. Though her eyes were open and her breaths coming even and easy, she did not respond.

"She ain't talked since it happened. Madame says she's in shock."

"Did the man in black do this to her?"

"No," our guide said. "She did. She did it to herself. Down below, too. She used a pair of sewing scissors. We couldn't stop her."

Hawking was content to approach no closer, but I needed to see what the man in black had done. I took a moment to consider what the young woman had told me, then another moment to move aside the bandages only enough to see the wounds. Bone shone through on her cheeks and jaws, sundered muscle peeling out. She did not grimace, though if she had, I would not have been able to tell. I choked, and closed my eyes, and in that moment relived seeing your father's viscera shoot forth from his body on the porch. It was the handiwork of the same monster.

After adjusting the bandages and feeling Grace's forehead with the back of my hand, I looked to my companion. He was chewing his lip for want of tobacco, but his eyes were mostly clear. Aside from fixing up a poultice to ensure she would not succumb to blood fever, we could do little for her.

Then something behind me drew Hawking's eyes beyond my shoulder.

Grace called my name. My name, as my mother had given it to me rather than as my neighbors had pressed it together. My eyes widened, while Hawking frowned but did not otherwise react. I turned towards the cot, bracing myself for the worst. Behind me, the door hinges squawked. Our guide had had her fill and bolted out of the room.

"Li Lian," Grace said again, all but singing it.

I stared back at her, uncertain if I were speaking to the girl, or to another using her as a conduit. In either case, the hairs on my arms stood tall, and a cold current ran from my tailbone to my throat. Never in my life had I seen a girl with eyes so black as hers.

"He says he'll see you in St. Louis."

II

NOT UNTIL WE EMERGED from the brothel did I realize I had been holding my breath. I paid the girl for her time
and considered but did not offer to heal her friend's face. A
dark channel had opened up between Grace and me, and I did
not want whatever was on the other side of it to reach across
and grab me. Or you.

"How in the hell did she know your name?" Hawking asked.

"I don't know," I said.

"While we're at it, how does HE know your name?"

"I don't know," I said again.

My mind was on the implication of the monster's reaching through that young prostitute's body to speak to me. Could
very well have been that he had told Grace to say that to me,
that he was trying to frighten me home. That would mean he
was just a man, though. And I could tell from looking sidelong
at Hawking that even he did not believe that.

The roadhouse had stood for so long unaccosted due to the solidarity of the women who tended it. Your great-grandmother had long since passed, and once we girls had all grown and left the house, so had Aunt Lucinda. Only my mother and Aunt Griselda remained behind to tend to the hearth and grant shelter to those seeking it. Your gran Cat would bundle herbs and brew tinctures and tonics for those who asked, and your great-aunt Griselda would read their cards and their palms and reveal their futures within. That they had each other had been a comfort to me all these years, but I felt no comfort now, only fear and pain.

I had no notion of the nature or character of the monster who had killed your father and was now threatening the rest of my family. Though I had my suspicions, the books from which I drew them were hundreds of miles upriver.

At the time, I made no notice of it, as the butcher's moods had a tendency to fluctuate depending upon how much whiskey he managed to put away before unconsciousness came to claim him. I know now, looking back, that he was in a darker mood than I had seen thus far. I was not interested in his mood, whether it was singular or shifting. I now knew the way from Madame Lavoie's to the hotel on Dauphine Street, and I moved as quickly as my bare feet and belly allowed.

"Wake the stabler," I said as we rounded the corner towards the hotel. The street still stank of blood and burnt gunpowder.

Hawking neither questioned me nor responded with his usual brand of insolence. He patted down his person to assure himself he had not misplaced his wallet, then left me to my errand.

I rushed through the lobby and past the saloon, where the clinking glassware and shuffling cards would have been a siren song to my companion had he accompanied me inside. Packing was among the least of my concerns. The mirror at the vanity table, however, I went straight to, pushing the dainty chair out of the way and bracing myself on the table.

My mother's Work has always been enabled by the use of mirrors, but I learned to extend my sight through minerals, black obsidian, and the sediment at the bottom of a copper cup. This mattered not one lick to me. I wanted to reach out to my mother, and my Will was stronger than my tools would have been.

I looked into the mirror, breathing slow and purposeful until all that existed was my intention to summon my mother. If the spell had succeeded, the reflection would have rippled and your gran would have appeared, and I would have sent her the message I kept in the back of my mind.

It did not succeed. I was quite calm by the time I realized she would not come, but I could not bring her to the mirror.

The door slammed open a moment later and Hawking leaned in to ask, "What are you doing?"

"Trying to send a message to my mother," I said. "There's too much water."

"Why don't you send her a telegram and save yourself a headache?"

"Telegram?"

He stared at me a moment, then sighed and scrubbed his face with his hand.

"Christ," he said. "Come on."

To my eye, the telegraph station was no different than any of the other buildings I had seen in the business district thus far. It was not quite so large, and it boasted a porch where the other buildings did not seem to invite their patrons to sit and stay awhile. This time of night, any who might have been so inclined had already found their diversions and committed to them. Our horses encountered no traffic as they clopped along.

All of the station's windows were darkened, and the front door resisted intrusion. I found, at last, a sign that said *Back at dawn*, hung upon a more permanent fixture that stated the establishment was open all night.

When I turned to voice my displeasure to Hawking, he was nowhere to be seen. I called his name, and received no answer. I called louder, and only the horses responded. One shook out her mane and snorted while the other pawed the ground and nickered. Though I did not speak their language, I took it for an attempt to communicate all the same and went back to the cart. What I muttered to the animals as I dug through my slap-dash medicine bag does not bear repeating, but in my digging I found a white ribbon and a book of matches. Though I had him on my mind already, I breathed steady to dispel my impatience before I introduced flame to the fabric.

Once the spell was cast, I tied the horses to the post out front and told them to behave themselves while I was gone. The foggy trail illuminating Hawking's way hung low to the ground and did not proceed in a straight line. It wavered from side to side, a trait I would have taken for injury had I not known my prey.

It was no path I would have thought to follow if I had to think as Hawking was thinking. It took me south, through open plots of land and long stretches of lit yet empty streets. Were it not for the persistence of the ribbon's trail, I would have thought myself to be imagining the distance he had covered. Thinking back, I ought not have been surprised.

At first I was uncertain of where he had gone, for the place was contained by a weary metal fence with neither signs nor light to see by. The ground was parched and the grass had died, and while the earth itself had a reverent quality, I could tell the church had not sanctified the place. Such places have an airless quality about them, a sense of being alone and being watched at the same time. I have been inside a church only once, my cousins and I daring each other to see who would be brave enough to run into one after nightfall and run back out again. None of us burst into flames, but we wished we had when our mothers found out what we had done.

Just because the entity described in the Christian Bible is a fiction does not mean spirits do not exist. They do. Whatever Christians summon when they give their sermons and perform their rituals, I am not familiar with. But in this place, I recognized its absence. The land felt abandoned.

I realized then that Hawking had approached the graveyard from the north. We were standing in a potter's field.

Unlike those of a consecrated cemetery, the graves were marked by modest stones if they were marked at all, and to see from one end to the other was hardly a task. I did not have to follow the ribbon's trail the rest of the way, for I saw my friend crouched down in front of a small gray slab. Or perhaps he was sitting. My memory has afforded him more dignity than his due.

Regardless, Hawking did not hear me approach, not because my steps were light but because he was absorbed in his own ritual. A fresh bottle of whiskey sat at his side. The stone had a smooth face and rough edges. Over his shoulder, I read the inscription:

MAY GOD GRANT YE MERCY

Without a name or dates, I could only look upon the stone and the man sat in front of it. I opened my mouth to draw him back from the precipice, but decided against it in the end. When he was ready, he would come find me, or I would leave without him.

Dawn was still a way off as I began my slow journey from the cemetery back to the telegraph station. Boys with newspapers piled high on the backs of their bicycles and men in white uniforms driving clanging milk carts passed me from time to time. I and a lone woman I presumed by her dress and the focus of her eyes to be a midwife passed each other by. She smiled at me, and I at her.

The horses were where I had left them, if a bit cross that I had left them, and I hung their oat bags and offered them apples from my hand. They would not forget my abandonment, but they would forgive it for the moment. While they ate I took a seat in one of the wicker chairs on the station's porch and watched the sun rise.

Not long after a neighborhood rooster began to crow, the windows slid upward and the shutters slid outward and the front door jingled and opened. I turned to glimpse the owner, or at least what I presumed was the owner, which may have been a poor presumption on my part.

He was the shortest grown man I had ever seen in my life, with wisps of spun-sugar hair covering a perfectly round head as well as the knuckles of his hands, which themselves were liberally liver-spotted. Though his spine was stooped with age and his hands shook, he was quick on his feet and quicker with a grin. Some of his teeth had left behind pink holes, but he did not appear to miss them.

"*Bonjour!*" he said, and then repeated himself, his accent even thicker than Madame Lavoie's. "*Entrez, entrez, je viens de terminer le nettoyage de notre telegraph d'impression!*"

"I'm sorry," I said. "I don't speak French."

"That is fine!" he said. "I do not speak English! Hah!"

Whether he was mad or just pulling my leg, I forced a smile and attempted to play the part of the gracious patron.

"You have send a telegraph before, *n'est-ce pas?*"

"No," I said. "Not exactly."

He walked me to the counter and spoke the entire way about the telegraph.

In spite of my hesitation, he told me of the English inventor Francis Ronalds, who built the first working telegraph in 1816 and powered it with static electricity, setting up an underground trench 175 yards long and an 8-mile-long overhead line. At the ends of the lines were revolving dials marked with the letters of the alphabet, and the electrical impulses sent along the wire, carefully tapped out by the operator, would spell out a message a single letter at a time. Not until twenty years later would American scientist David Alter invent the electric telegraph in Pennsylvania. Though he demonstrated its use to witnesses, he, unlike Samuel Morse the next year in 1837, never attempted to patent the idea.

"Do you know," the telegraphist asked, "that the first message he send, in 1844, from Washington to Baltimore, say, 'What hath God wrought??'"

"I did not," I said.

Behind him lurked the machine, a monstrosity of keys and wheels and wires set up on a stately wooden desk, with tendrils sneaking up the ceiling and out into the beyond. Apparently there was another one just like it in St. Louis. Whatever I wrote down for the telegraphist to send, another man whose face I may well have never seen would transcribe it, and read it, and only after all of that would he contact my mother.

Part of me longed to see her face, to tell her myself what had happened to your father. I wanted my mother the way I fear you will want me and I will not be there. Another part of me felt the wild teenager in need of reproach as soldiers hauled her back from Texas. But I did not care. All I cared was to know she was alive, and it was only the water or distance or some other unknown keeping me from reaching her.

Above all else, I had to warn her.

Behind the counter, the telegraphist had wet the nib of his pen and introduced it to a well of ink and was now looking at me, one eye a clear brown and the other clouded by cataract.

"*Êtes-vous prête?*" he asked.

It was not until that moment that I realized how strange the message would be to this man. It seemed unwise that I tell him I was a pregnant fugitive witch chasing a mysterious stranger who'd killed my husband and whom I had on good authority from a self-mutilating prostitute was on his way to do harm to my sorceress kin in St. Louis. Even if I could use my Will on him, it would not affect the man who received the message in St. Louis and thought it nonsense or worse.

I nodded, gave him a weak "Yes," and began in the form instructed: "Matthew dead by what you feared."

"Matthieu dead as by what you feared. *Arrêt.*" His mind caught up to his hands, and I saw sadness in his gaze as he looked at me through his stormy eye. "Matthieu, he was your husband?" he asked, with his eyes on you. I nodded. *"Mes condoléances."*

My dear, strange though it seems, aside from Hawking, this stranger was the first person to express sympathy for your father's passing. This man who had never met us seemed to genuinely care about our fate. He motioned for me to continue.

"Sought by Ness," I said in a tone I hoped would dispel suspicion.

He looked up. "A suitor, so soon?"

"Yes, well, he's certainly after me," I said. Before he could ask another question, I went on, "In New Orleans. Fear this darkness coming for you next." His sadness persisted, but otherwise the man did not appear alarmed. "You will need strong wards. On way by riverboat."

After the old telegraphist returned the pen to the inkwell, he held it up and blew on it and counted the words. As he calculated the cost on a wooden abacus beside a metal cash register that may well have been older than he was, he did not speak.

It was not the clearest warning, but given the circumstances and your father's death, I thought your gran would see its meaning in spite of the murk.

I do not know whether Hawking had chosen to wait for me outside, or if he had decided to sit there until he reached the bottom of the bottle. I did not ask. I came out of the telegraph station, and I saw him in the wicker chair I had occupied not so long before. This time of day I was prepared for him to be uselessly drunk, and perhaps he was. But his drunkenness was often accompanied by jokes, or questions, or some other manner of nonsense that only strengthened my desire to see him swiftly off to sleep.

He took a deep breath when he saw me and braced himself on either arm of the chair. When he stood, he did not wobble. His eyes were reddened. Though I looked at him long enough to judge him fit to continue on, I did not ask him what was the matter.

"You send your message?" he slurred.

"I did."

"You ready?"

"I am."

"Good," he said, and began an uneven walk towards the street. "I found a man who wants to buy the horses."

"You've been busy," I said.

He had nothing to say to that. He started readying the horses to walk, and I stole a moment to pet Matthew's, the one he had named and I had teased him for naming. It was an uncomplicated process. After we signed the animals over to the broker, he paid us in large bills and we made our unhurried way to the riverboat landing.

I do not recall much about our time on the steamboat. It was a large, sturdy vessel with plenty of room both above and below deck, such that anyone who did not wish an encounter with another person could easily avoid one. For my part, I was both restless and exhausted. The steamboat afforded us a place to rest and meals at sunup and sundown, and our first full day on the river I availed myself of all they offered. Something told me I would not have much rest in the days to come, and I took as much as I could.

Our second night on the river, I awakened for no discernible reason and did so to an empty cabin. This would not strike me as unusual but for the fact of Hawking's behavior striking me as strange. He had said very little to me after we left Madame Lavoie's, and I could not enjoy the silence for its sounding to me like a warning.

Well past dark, likely nearing midnight, I made my way above deck in a nightgown and a pair of moccasins I had pur-chased from another couple traveling all the way to Saint Paul, Minnesota. My feet were thick with callouses and had never grown accustomed to shoes, but I wore them anyway. I feared slipping and hurting you.

A short walk around the steamboat's deck revealed Hawking standing at its stern, polishing off what I feel safe in assuming was another new bottle of whiskey. He had a weak grip on the railing that suggested he was hoping to go over, not retain his balance.

"Roger," I said to get his attention rather than to chastise him.

"What," he said.

"You're making me nervous."

"Ah, I ain't gonna jump."

"Were you thinking about it?"

"Course I was thinking about it." He sighed and turned away from the water as I settled beside him. He went on, "I'm too pigeon-livered to kill myself. Always have been."

"It don't take courage to kill yourself," I said.

"Well, whatever it takes, I ain't got. I've let other people die, you know, to pay for what I've done."

"Would you quit feeling sorry for yourself?" I asked. "I owe you a debt I can never repay. You're risking your own neck right now just being with me. That takes courage."

He snorted, took another long pull off the bottle, and squinted at it once he realized it was empty. Into the black water it went, hitting with a hollow splash before the current and the churning backwash from the boat made off with it.

"You got any spells that can erase memories?" he asked.

"I could," I said.

"Would you, if I asked you to?"

Given the state he was in, I would not feel justified in prying what he wanted gone out of him, nor in wiping away whatever he thought he could no longer live with. Maybe if he were sober when he asked, but at that juncture I had more faith in the man in black turning himself in than I had in Hawking drying out.

I said, "I know something's hurting you. I could work a spell to make you forget it. Thing is, the past hurts sometimes. You either learn from the hurt, or you run from it. I make you forget, you got nothing left to learn from. You'll always be running, and you won't know why. You hear me?"

"I hear you," he said, though he did not sound convinced.

"Come on inside," I said. "Sleep on it. Come morning, you still want me to make you forget, you go on ahead and ask. I owe you that much."

"In the morning?"

"That's right."

"You promise?"

"I promise."

He nodded and let me put a hand on his back to steady him as we made our way back below deck. As he had at the hotel, he fell asleep as if he and sleep were long lost to each other, but this time he acquiesced to taking off his boots and suspenders first.

That night I would relive in my dreams the night your father died, but it was at the roadhouse, and it was your Nana Cat the man in black shot on the porch instead. I lay awake, holding you, whispering spells of protection for you, and her, and your father's spirit, wherever it was.

In the morning, Hawking mentioned neither our talk nor our agreement. I reckon he had decided the memory of his trespass, whatever it was, was his punishment to endure. I waited the whole rest of the trip, but we made it to the docks in St. Louis without him breathing a word of it.

12

THE CITY OF MY BIRTH appeared as a faint speck growing larger as the boat churned up the water between our location and destination. I fought against the urge to dive overboard and swim to shore. That I could not reach my mother nor determine the location of the men we had followed so far south to begin with had made my sleep as restless as my companion's. It was not what lay behind me that troubled me so much as it was the unknown before us.

Hawking's spirits improved the further north we carried, as if we were on opposite ends of a scale. By the time the captain gave the order to let down the gangway, I was all but delirious with need, pushing my way through the crowd of passengers.

"Christ on a cross, would you slow your ass down?" Hawking said as I hurried to the main road, leaving him to drag what few effects we still had in our possession after the sale of the horses to pay for the boat ticket.

I did not slow down. I thrust my arms in the air to catch the attention of a waiting stagecoach driver and told him where we needed to go and how quickly we needed to do so.

The driver gave my wild hair a curious look, but did not question me further. He took the luggage from Hawking, who helped me into the back of the coach, and I cannot recall what we discussed, if anything at all. All I can tell you is the city of my childhood passed by as a blur I had no interest in sharpening.

By the time the coach pulled up to the roadhouse's front drive, I had all but made myself sick with anticipation. The sickness that afflicts many women in the early days of their pregnancy had never bothered me, and it was not come to haunt me in the later ones. All I had left in this world, my family and my history and the things I had left behind in legacy, the roadhouse had kept safe.

Its front door was wide open, though the curtains for the saloon were drawn and the sign flipped to say CLOSED.

Without waiting for Hawking, I scrambled down from the coach and ran up the dirt path leading from the paved street to our porch. In my wake I left a trail of little wildflowers, which I know caused my companion to heave a hard sigh. I paid his consternation no mind. What mind I had left was on the other side of the threshold.

As I passed through it, I noticed the door's glass inlay was cracked from one corner to its opposite. The CLOSED sign hung askew.

I called for my mother before my feet met the welcome mat, and I heard a commotion that would have provoked me to draw my weapon had I thought to bring one with me. All I had were my bare hands, and I felt the tingling in my fingers that forewarned an invocation of my Will. Then the voices became familiar to me, and I recognized the cadence of the footsteps.

Eva, her belly grown bigger than mine with her third pregnancy, stepped out of the kitchen as quickly as she could and still maintain her balance. Her hands took hold of my elbows as if in preparation to embrace me, but her eyes were wild and brimming with salt water.

"Oh, thank Cailleach you're alive," said my cousin. She embraced me, as close as two women carrying children can.

"What's happened?" I asked. "Where's my mother?"

"She's not here, Lily."

Only through my imagination could I see the roadhouse as it should have been. As it was, the bar glittered with shattered glassware. I saw the man in black gripping your gran by the scalp and hauling her across it, glass chewing up her face. I saw blood on the ground and imagined him savaging her with his ungloved fists. I saw chairs and rope and looked away.

When I returned to the present, Eva was standing firm to keep me from passing down the corridor.

"What's in the kitchen, Eva?"

Eva shook her head no.

"Eva, what's in the kitchen?"

I looked to the threshold, where Hawking had dragged our luggage and now stood like a creature of the night, unable to enter without invitation. I left Hawking in the entryway, moving my distraught cousin aside and following the familiar corridor past the stairwell and the saloon's double doors until I came to the sunken kitchen, which smelled of rendered fat and singed hair. My cousins Agnes and Charlotte stood around the great table in the center of the kitchen with horror having drained the color from their cheeks.

Laid out in the center of the table were limbs. Two arms and two legs, slender and discolored, with a long silver braid serving to close the pentagram. I could not help but gasp at the sight and cover my mouth with my hand, and I could not help but cry out when the realization hit me. The limbs were older and thinner than I remembered, but I recognized them. They were those of my aunt Griselda.

"Lily," said Charlotte, her voice wavering but her tears yet unshed.

"Where's the rest of her?" I asked.

"What?"

"Her HEAD, Charlie. What did he do with her head?"

Charlotte shook her head to indicate she did not know, and I let the matter lie. Your cousins knew little more than I did.

It would not occur to me until later, when I confided as much in Hawking, that my travels and years on the frontier had toughened me. Agnes, with her interest in men, and Charlotte, with her interest in maps and far-flung places, were lacking my experience, and Eva had always wanted to grow up and become a mother herself above all else.

I love my cousins dearly. Their lives are their own, and though we do not want the same things, they are tough and smart and kind, in their own ways. Knowing they will be influences in your life, that you and Eva's sons will grow up together, gives me comfort I know I do not deserve.

All the same—our childless, tale-weaving, sharp-tongued auntie Griselda was dead. Your gran was captured, strung up, enduring treatment I could only imagine. We had to do something.

As the eldest daughter, when her mother died, your gran moved out of her bedroom at the back of the house and into the carriage house on the other side of the garden. If I had stayed, I would have inherited the room. I do not know whose room it was, in my absence. It was made up as if in expectation of a guest, but it neither appeared nor felt as though anyone truly lived in it.

I felt the eyes of my cousins on my back as I passed through the garden where I had spent so many sunny afternoons as a child, several of the shrubs and fronds trampled under the intruders' heavy steps. Agnes called after me, and I ignored her. I let myself into the carriage house, tidy and full of my mother's energy, candles and cobwebs and bundles of herbs in their proper places.

She had left a nightgown at the end of the tightly made bed, doubtless with the intent to hang it in her wardrobe before the interruption tore her away from her routine. I picked up the nightgown, burying my face in its fabric and breathing deep in the hopes of catching a particle through which I could focus my search.

Your Nana Catriona is the strongest woman I know. She is built tall and fine, though her life's pursuits have added toughness to her skin and her bones. Her hair retains some of its red even in her advancing age. She would be able to send a message even with great interference, while I had to find a conduit through which to reach her. That she had not reached out to me in all this time left my stomach awash in ice water. For the first time since stepping off the boat, I felt fear of a sort I will do everything left in my power to ensure you never, ever, encounter.

One day you will see the Library. It is intact, even after everything that has come to pass, and every bit as grand as it was when I was a child. Grander perhaps for its having survived this assault. But at that moment, when I passed through the doors and came to stand in the same spot in which we all stood when beginning to question where we would begin in our pursuit of knowledge, I felt two warring presences.

My mother's presence was the strongest here, she being the eldest of our mothers and spending the most time here, but I felt it at war with that of the man in black. My revulsion

intensified as I looked upon the chaos he had made of our un-
spoken order.

When I was young, perhaps the age you are now reading
this, I could reach only the lower three shelves, and I believed
the Library to be far grander than it appears to me in adult-
hood. Thick curtains kept the sun and its rays from damaging
the pages, some of which had survived since our line first began
hundreds of years ago, and though the interior was dim and
packed full of furniture and instruments, not to mention books,
it felt vast rather than cramped.

There in one corner was Aunt Lucinda's abandoned altar to
the nature spirits, whom industry threatened to drive out forever.
There in another was Aunt Griselda's, her tarot cards stacked
neat, her minerals stacked even neater still. A spider had spun a
web over her table, connecting a lamp to a bookshelf. I know it
was not new—Griselda had treated spiders as messengers. My
mother did not keep her instruments in the Library. Hers were
behind the bar, in the attic of the carriage house. This place was
where group Work happened.

As a girl, my awareness of the Library ended at eye level,
until I realized I could use the power of my mind to remove
books from the higher shelves if I did not want to take the time
to position and climb the ladder. When I sat at the table cen-
tered between the only set of windows in the space, I treated it
as a desk and not as the altar that it truly is. The space smelled

of ashes and salt and time, of sage and lavender and the binding glue that holds books together for so many centuries.

By smell alone, I could almost believe I had come home. My other senses dispelled that notion. The man in black had let himself in, and he had stood in this most sacred of spaces, and I could tell without even beginning to look around that he had taken something we could not replace.

I began to make my way around the exterior of the Library, working shelf by shelf. My fingers drifted over titles I had once memorized, tomes about the power of True Names when dealing with adversaries, about the uses of herbs and minerals and elements and blood. Spells for fertility, spells for good fortune. Spells to affect the family, spells to affect the community, spells to bargain with the spirits and spells to bind them.

I found the dark spellbook my mother had warned me away from as a younger girl, the book written in Latin that had damned my ancestor Eimhir. Dark not because it dealt with hexes but because the spells violated so many natural laws. They could prolong life, return life, destroy life. But all that alteration came with a price. It was the darkest book in the Library. The rest of them, whether written in Latin or Gaelic or Arabic, as some of the very oldest books were written in, were books of theory and practical application. Which components worked for the caster who had taken pen to paper. For a moment I was a girl again, all of her future awaiting her still, rather than a widow.

This is where my mother sat me down when she had learned of my indiscretion in the schoolyard, encircling me in salt that no wandering spirits would take interest in my practice, and refusing to let me break the circle until I had demonstrated restraint. I would have made a room like this in our house on the prairie, would have let your father glimpse it on the occasions when his curiosity overtook him, but would never let him inside. He would never hear giggling or singing within its walls, for I would teach you early and young to be reverent in a space full of books and scrolls. Instead you will see the books and scrolls on your own, and you will know what it is to learn the history of witches and pagans from papyrus reams that survived the burning of the Library of Alexandria, and you will know why it is that men and the mundane are not allowed in such places in our family.

I was on the opposite side of the Library when the door groaned open, and I turned in preparation to fight before realizing it was Hawking.

"Good God," he said.

"You don't belong here," I told him. Then I realized it was not the Library itself that had drawn his words and followed his eyes to a high shelf.

There sat the head of your aunt Griselda.

In spite of Hawking's protests, I drew and climbed the ladder. The monster had wrenched open her jaws and crammed an old page into her mouth. After a moment to ensure I would not lose either the contents of my stomach or my composure, I descended the stairs of the ladder with one hand full, Hawking helping me down the last few rungs. I collapsed to the floor and held your great-aunt's head in my lap, refusing to cry.

I cannot now be certain of the exact wording of the page I extracted from Aunt Griselda's mouth, what with letters missing and it being written in Old English, but I will try:

Beware he who hunts with fire. He is minister to those with weak spirits, shepherd to those with empty hearts. Darkness commands him, and he wields it to command. His name echoes in the valley of shadows and he treads through centuries. His path is marked in blood. Those who follow do not return.

The urgency with which Hawking said my name and shook my shoulder was due to my having been lost in a fog.

"Woman, the law is going to be here before long. You gotta get up."

Until that moment, I had given only cursory thought to the fact that Ness might have alerted the authorities in St. Louis. I had not cared before, and I was not sure how much I cared anymore, but Hawking was right. I had to get up.

In the time I was gone, my cousins had gathered up the pieces desecrating the table in the center of the room and scrubbed away the blood. The scent of lye and burnt sage hung in the air. All the cleansing in our power would not undo what had happened here, and I saw determination in Eva's eyes as she worked at the table in spite of the memory staining its surface. They gasped at the sight of the head but I made no mention of the paper or warning.

I went into the pantry and found a bundle of dried thyme and a sprig of dried yarrow, both of which I brought to the table and ground together with a mortar and pestle. Though Eva looked at me from time to time, she continued her own Work without speaking. When I had finished, I poured the powder into my palm and carried it to the front door.

After dipping a finger into the powder and anointing my forehead with it, I tossed the palmful into the air and let it fall where it would. That the man in black had sought to conceal his path did not surprise me. I did not, however, expect that his path would appear just as the passage had warned.

His path was marked in blood.

I held a hand over you and followed the bloody footprints out of the foyer and onto the front porch, where they strode down the steps and along the dirt path. What flowers had sprung up in my wake were dying now that the man in black's presence was revealed. I crouched down next to one of the prints, wary of it even before I placed my palm in its center.

It was then my mind left my body.

When I blinked, my consciousness was no longer in an autumnal river town in Missouri but traveling across an open expanse of salt and shale. The ridges and cliffs faded in color from the blue black of a bruise to the vivid red of blood fresh from an artery. A breeze cut across the land and met no resistance, neither tree nor shrub nor flower to buffer its force. I thought I knew what howling wind was, hearing it whip across the plains in wintertime with nothing to stop it.

But the plains were alive. They sustained life. This was a soulless land that sustained nothing.

I knew of few places that featured such desolate landscapes. The scoria and sandstone and silence told me where the blood would lead.

When I took my hand away from the print, I did so with a gasp, my consciousness returning to my body all at once and bringing with it memory of the path my prey had taken. I heard Charlotte's voice behind me, felt her hands on my arm and shoulder, and once I was certain I was back in St. Louis, I let her help me to my feet.

With the autumn afternoon burning down, we had little time to discuss what we would do and how we would go about doing it. I knew I was tempting fate every moment I stayed, but the truth was the presence of your cousins was a comfort I needed so. That time was better spent putting Aunt Griselda's pieces together as best we could, laying her in the ground as best we could, joining hands in a circle in a gathering for the departed as best we could.

By the time we had set fire to her remains and broken our circle, dusk had fallen. My cousins agreed to stay at the roadhouse and keep the hearth warm in anticipation of my return.

I wish I could tell you they convinced me to stay, that Eva had told me what the ringing in her ears and the ache in her teeth told her. That she had even whispered it to Agnes, that she might act as the eldest, as the most mature of us. Agnes, who had never settled down with a man, who like as not never would, who drank and played cards and swore just the same as I did but who knew she was beautiful, who used her beauty as a focus for her Work.

Though my cousins Worked in their own way—Eva handing me a packet of tea leaves and a bag of corn biscuits she had blessed to keep the baby safe, Charlotte pricking the pad of my thumb and pressing the well of blood to her third eye that she would be able to See me and assist me in spite of the distance, and Agnes taking the box of ammunition Hawking had had no cause to use in all this time and enchanting the bullets that they would find their mark in his time of need—I would not let them convince me to stay.

Hawking and I bid our farewells, and we took Aunt Griselda's cart and Aunt Griselda's motherless horses to the trail that would lead us to the end of the world.

13

WE WERE ANOTHER MONTH on the road from St. Louis, Missouri, to the Badlands of the Nebraska Territory.

My dear, if ever you have reason to travel west of the Missouri River, keep in mind the wide expanses of untouched land lain between you and your destination. This country began its life as thirteen colonies on the eastern shores of a populous and inhabited land, and the borders have pushed ever westward so long as American soldiers have had bayonets and gunpowder. I have no doubt in my mind another war will come to pass before you are grown.

However difficult the journey had been on the way to New Orleans, the journey north was even more difficult still. To the fire kindled by grief, I had added unrelenting fear for your gran. I imagined her eyes blindfolded and her mouth gagged, her hands bound, slung over the back of a horse when she could no longer keep stubborn pace along the path. I imagined your father's killer tearing her into pieces as he had your great-aunt Griselda.

While I tormented myself with these thoughts, Hawking deteriorated. His hands shook even when he held on to the reins, and on more than one occasion he either climbed or collapsed down from the cart's front seat to empty his stomach, no doubt raw after a lifetime of heavy drinking. I suspected he did not want to be nursed, and so I did my best to ignore his sickness until it became an impediment to me.

"You can't just stop all at once," I said to him on the fourth day, when he was barely able to sit up on his own but insisted on doing so all the same.

"What are you talking about?" he asked.

"Drinking. You trying to kill yourself?"

"I'm fine."

"That dead rabbit we passed a few miles back looks better than you do."

"Darlin'," he said, "you say the sweetest damned things."

Taking my heavy sigh as an indication of waning patience, he allowed me to stop the wagon early and start a fire that I could brew a tea made from milk thistle and nettle. This I added to a two-quart glass jar I had brought along for a similar purpose, along with enough whiskey as to cause the average person to become sick for the opposite reason. When I was through, I handed him the jar and told him to drink it.

Though he griped, Hawking allowed me to continue driving the wagon while he rested. By the time he had finished the jar, considerable color had returned to his gaunt cheeks and his stomach had settled enough that he could take in solid food.

He steadied himself and turned to me.

"Lilian," Hawking said, "I'm not sure I ever knew what this little mission of ours was about. That man shot me and killed Matthew. You were trapped in that cell, and Ness was going to see you hang, and that didn't sit right with me. But I never really played it out."

"Well, you should've," I said. "Now ain't the time."

"Do you even know what we're chasing?"

"Shut up, Hawk. I mean it."

"I'll tell you what I know," he said.

"Don't," I said.

"I know whatever we're chasing ain't a man, and I know what happened that night wasn't about someone getting angry at the doc for not being able to mend a leg."

"Please, Hawk."

"He's been baiting us. He's been baiting *you*. Ever since De Soto. We ain't chasing him, he's letting us follow him, and it ain't cause he has plans for you to avenge Matt's death or save your ma."

I regret how I treated Hawking next, but I was not ready to contemplate what lay ahead, and anger came to me easier than understanding.

"Was she your wife?"

"What?" he asked.

"The potter's field in New Orleans. I followed you."

Hawking drew a deep breath, his jaws tight for a moment. Though he said nothing, I persisted.

"How did she die?"

"Natural causes," he said. A long pause followed, and I held my tongue in anticipation of the truth. "Once upon a time," he said, "in a little town called New Orleans, there lived a butcher and his wife. The butcher had inherited his business from his stepfather, a mean son of a bitch who died with more debt than even his accountant had known about, and while the butcher found this revelation distressing, the butcher's wife was much calmer about the matter. She assured him the Lord never gives a man more burden than he can bear, and besides, she loved him.

"Well, the butcher had a bit of a love affair with gambling, and long story short, he soon found himself not only still very much in debt to the bank but to a bad man who, it was generally agreed upon, nobody in the city wanted to owe money to. The butcher was in quite a bit of hot water, but his wife told him not to worry. They'd figure something out.

"Well, the butcher kept on gambling, figuring if he kept splashing coin around on the table he would have to break even one of these nights. He didn't break even. He got himself further into debt than he already was, and since he couldn't pay up once he lost, his associates told him, 'Sorry, pal, you're not welcome here anymore. Try someplace else. Come back when your credit's good again.'

"Wouldn't you know it, the last place in the whole city where the butcher's money was any good was this little whorehouse in Storyville run by a Madame Chantal Lavoie."

Hawking cleared his throat, and though I suspected he would leave the story unfinished, he did not.

"She was there. I went out of my damned mind, got tossed out by a couple of Lavoie's kept men. Next time I saw her, she was hanging from a beam in the attic. Left me a note and a box full of cash, enough to pay off the rest of the debt and then some. Coroner said the baby in her belly'd been there since before she started whoring."

We observed a spell of silence, he having said all he cared to say and I feeling uncertain of what to say myself. Condolences would not do my thoughts justice, and Hawking would have laughed at my pity, anyway.

So I let the silence run its course and then I asked, "That why you giving up drinking? You drinking ain't got nothing to do with my failing Matt."

"Bah," said Hawking, and spat in the road. "You didn't fail your man, and we ain't failing now, neither. We're going to find the bastard, Lilian. And I intend to be sober when we do."

"I don't know who he is, Hawk," I said. "I don't know where he came from. I don't know why he killed Matthew. I don't know what control he has over others, or why he chose me, or if we're going to find him before he finds us."

"Does it matter?"

The absence of an answer was an answer on its own.

"You could turn back," he said. "It's a big country."

"Don't matter how big it is. Did you forget I'm wanted for murdering my husband? The lawman chasing after me was his best friend. If he finds me before I find this man, he's promised me the courtesy of letting me give birth in a jail cell before they hang me, so he can raise my child as his. And he won't stop until he does find me. So there ain't no way out except through."

"So that's it."

"He killed my husband. He took my mother. Whether we're hunting him or he's baiting us, ain't no way this ends without our paths crossing. So yeah, Hawk, that's it."

We traveled in silence for a time, my blood up and Hawking's spirits down. Before I could grow accustomed to it, Hawking broke it.

"'Died in a bullet storm' makes a better tombstone, anyway."

14

DE LA CRUZ WAS HIDING in a shack out in the Badlands.

This I saw from the back of the cart, with only a waxing crescent moon for light. I filled a small clay bowl with water from the river we had crossed one week earlier, and I dropped into the water pebbles and two leaves I had picked up intact along the riverbed, and I pricked my finger with a sewing needle I disinfected with whiskey from the butcher's reserves. The blood spoke of my intent. If my intent were unjust, I do not believe the water would have shown me an image of de la Cruz stirring stew over a low cook fire. I do not believe the leaves would have turned in their bath to show me the way to begin walking, nor continued to point that way once I had begun.

By now I trust you believe magick is a fickle thing. It can be. Or perhaps it is only so fickle as the one practicing its ways. But for as much of the world as I have cared to see and as easy as I have found it to leave the place I once thought of as home,

I do not believe this makes me a fickle creature myself. No more than the wind is fickle, or the trees or the waters.

I did not know the exact way to take to reach de la Cruz from the road, or rather the bone-dry expanse of sand we chose to call the road, but I did know the ways around not knowing the way. How to find signs of life and match the signs to the life one hopes to find. So we drove the cart as far into the Badlands as the horses could go with the terrain as uneven as it was, and when the rocks threatened to crack the cart's axle, we left the cart and the horses. It was not ideal for the beasts to stand in the dark, as they would bolt and take the cart with them if they spooked, but I tied their reins to a stump and left them there anyway. Reassurances of my return were like as not hollow when I took the only source of light with me.

The lantern I had found scarce need for until this night. This and the rifle we took from the back of the cart, and the butcher held the lantern while I wrapped my shawl around my shoulders and twined the divining leaves into a pendant that I hung around my neck.

"So what's your plan?" Hawking asked before we set off into the valley.

"I'm going to knock on the door," I said, "and he and I are going to have ourselves a chat, and he is going to tell me where I can find the man who killed my husband and took my mother."

"You're so sure about that."

"No," I said. "I ain't."

"How do you know you ain't going to walk in there and find our friend waiting to dispatch your mother like—"

My glare stopped him. "She ain't there. I'd have felt it. And neither is he." I considered Hawking and his hollowness in the light of what I now knew about him. "You should stay with the horses and cover me."

"I ain't aiming to stay here while you get yourself shot."

"Well, then, steady your hands," I said.

"Hah."

"And watch your mouth," I said. "He's outnumbered and he's got himself an itchy trigger finger, besides."

"Yeah, yeah," Hawking said.

When your father and I first moved to the Nebraska Territory, the way was not well known to us, and we had to trust our path and our safety in the thin maps drawn by those who had come before us and those we met along the way. I can recall feeling safer for knowing both your father and his rifle were there. Safety is nothing for which I would barter liberty, but that I have known at least the illusion of it in the past I count as a blessing.

I knew this night I was headed into territory man had not yet charted. If an outlaw were to seek refuge in this place, he would have to have met and learned it while the sun still shone. The pendant about my neck had lifted from my bosom and pointed straight in the direction I was to go. As I walked, my nearness to the Mexican gave it ease. It lowered with time, and before it returned to lying against my chest, I saw dim firelight burning through a window in the distance.

In the darkness I knelt, and Hawking extinguished the lantern before he began to creep forward. I too crept forward, as low to the ground as I could with the weight of you in my hips. Neither of us wore spurs or carried keys, and the only person who could feel you moving was me, yet the desolation of the landscape was so stark that I was aware of every sound, felt the tapping of our bootsoles on the rocky earth or your dancing around beneath my ribs was loud as a shout. So complete was the darkness, I could no longer see the pendant made of leaves. When I began to drift away from the house, I knew because I felt its shifting. Never have I so wished for a weapon beyond my own hands.

I stopped moving and felt for a boulder I could use for support and found one sturdy in the dark. I could feel de la Cruz out there.

Until that moment, I had not thought of whether I would recognize the cadence of the man's steps, having heard them just the once, and in a state of alarm at that. I could not hear him moving even when I strained to listen. I heard Hawking as he crept farther away, his intent to flank de la Cruz clear.

A rock popped as de la Cruz circled around the boulder I had chosen and set the pendant to turning. My eyes were soon adjusted to the darkness, and I wanted to reach for the lantern Hawking had left behind, but I did not want to alert de la Cruz to my location. We stayed like this for a time, long enough I felt as if the pendant had become a timepiece, its movement keeping with his circling around my location, neither of us daring to speak first.

I heard the clattering of his rifle's mechanisms as he pulled back the hammer. He was nearer to me than I thought he was. His accent and hatred stained his voice. This was the man who had lied straight to your father's face, who I counted just as responsible for the murder as the monster who had actually done the shooting.

"I know you're here," he said. "I can smell you."

My dear, I wanted to hurt him then. The way he spoke to the darkness and the way he moved in it as if it and he were of a kind. To kill a man with magick is no task to take on lightly. It is difficult enough to do good with it, and to kill a man takes something from the soul of the one who does the taking. At that moment my fatigue was in part due to the demands of pregnancy and so much time on the road but in part, also, because I was preparing to kill the man with a hex.

"You show yourself," said Lorenzo Chavez de la Cruz, "and I will not shoot you. I will shoot you if you make me come and find you. ¿Comprendes?"

If he were the sort of man to shoot at a woman heavily pregnant, then he would deserve whatever happened to him after that. This may seem to you a fair bit of recklessness, but in that moment you have to understand I was more concerned with what would happen to you than what would happen to me.

I stood from where I had crouched behind the boulder and held my palms so the Mexican could see they were empty and left the lantern on the ground behind me. Though I wore a medicine bag tied to the hem of my tunic and the pointing pendant around my neck, I knew he would not believe me unarmed otherwise. My hair was dirty and so was my face. If he thought I was there to kill him, I would not fault him, but I was not there to punish him for his thoughts.

"Who are you?" he asked.

"You don't recognize me," I said.

He was pointing the muzzle of his rifle in my direction, but I do not believe he had a true shot. Not in the dark and not with a flintlock weapon. Covered in dirt as I was, I could have called upon the dirt covering his palms and created heat. Made the weapon such as he could no longer hold on to it. This was an effort, and I began to make the effort.

"Nah," he said. "Now I do. You're the doctor's woman."

"What are you skulking around in the dark for?" I asked.

"I could ask you the same."

"Well," I said, "I was aiming to knock on the door and introduce myself proper."

"¿*Claro?*" he said with a hint of cruel amusement in his tone.

"It was. Suppose it could still be."

"Well, I suppose now I have to invite you in."

"I suppose so, too. Unless you want to talk about your boss out here in the open."

He lowered his rifle. In the dark I could see how he was breathing. Had been breathing all that time. He was agitated by the implication of my presence, but I could not determine whether that agitation would give way to violence easy or not.

"*Por el amor del cielo,*" he said. "Come inside."

I took him up on the offer so much as I felt it was no real offer at all. My options were few. If I stayed outside, he would shoot me. So I went inside.

The place was clean but dust covered everything, as if the cleaning had occurred before a great absence, and when I breathed in deep I could not smell so much the fireplace or what he had been cooking in the fireplace but the passage of time and the smell of impending death. He had not even swept the entryway the last time he entered. I could see the tracks made in the gray by his boots, and by something else having been dragged across the floor.

On the very far side of the room was a single bed with a pallet mattress. Lying on that mattress was the still form of Kelly Mackey, buried underneath blankets and breathing the uneven, lurching breaths of a dying man. What your father said back in De Soto had come to pass. That leg of his had turned to gangrene.

If the man in black were capable of even a sliver of mercy, he would have shot Mackey before shooting your father. Maybe that was what the men were hollering about, before Hawking and I interrupted them. I would not get the chance to ask. I had not come here for Mackey.

My attention shifted from the dying man on the bed to the metal in the stock of the Mexican's rifle, which he rested on the floor beside the fireplace. He flexed both of his hands once the weight was gone from them, and without touching them I knew they were thick with calluses and powerful.

"If you value your life," said de la Cruz after he closed the door, "you will cease looking for George Dalton, and you will go back home."

"My husband is dead," I said. "Y'all shot him."

"You were not there. You do not know what happened."

"I was there enough to hear it."

"George Dalton is evil."

"So I'd gathered."

"No," said de la Cruz, looking right at me as he sat himself down at the table and began to roll a cigarette. "No, I do not think you understand."

I said, "Them girls you had back in New Orleans made it sound like he was the devil, making them do things."

"And you do not believe them."

"Course I don't believe them. Ain't no such thing as the devil."

"But you do believe in demons."

"Spirits, sure. Not the Christian devil."

"If I tell you that George Dalton is very old, older than this country, you will say what?"

Everything in this world, and immortality is one of them, comes with a price. Spirits are just as liable to fade away as anything else. Without feeding from the memories of their living kin, they have to subsist on the desperation of strangers. At least, that was what I thought I knew about spirits as I stood talking to de la Cruz.

I said, "I would say I'm curious to know what you mean by that. By my count that'd make him nigh unto a hundred years old, and he don't look even half that."

"Older," said de la Cruz.

He began to pick his nails with the tip of a heavy-handled knife, and I eyed the blade a moment before speaking again.

"You'll understand if I'm having trouble believing this," I said.

"Believe, or do not believe," he said. "It is all the same to him."

I asked, "How long you and Mackey been riding with him?"

He said, "Mackey we picked up in Kansas City some time ago. We needed a man who was good with the horses, and he did not ask questions. No family, neither. No parents, no woman, no *niños*. I do not think he was ever with a woman. He owed a lot of people money, was very bad at gambling. Too trusting."

"And what about you?"

"What about me?"

"You really expect me to believe the devil shot my husband?"

"Not the devil," said Chavez. *"El diablo es un cuento, nada más."*

"Un cuento," I said, scoffing. A story. "So you expect me to believe Mackey, who you brung into my house with a shot gut and a mangled leg, went from being just about dead when I left y'all alone with my husband to standing up, walking, talking, all on account of a demon who was compelling the rest of you bastards to do what y'all done, and this don't make you even bat an eye."

"You wish to know what happened?"

It brings me no shame to tell you I lost my composure then. I told him yes, I wished, so full of fervor that tears came to my eyes and I do believe he thought my labor pains had begun. If he thought this, it did not change the manner in which he spoke to me, and for that I grant the son of a bitch some measure of manhood. He offered me neither refreshment nor repose. We kept to our stances, he in front of the fire and I with my back to the door, and after a moment to catch both of our breaths, he doffed his hat from his head and laid it over the barrel of his gun. Dragged his hand down his face and I could see that he was sweating.

"Tell me," I said. "Please."

"There is not so much to tell," he said, and lit a cigarette to keep him company throughout the telling. "He disappeared for a time, when we were in California, and when he comes back, he says he knows the location of a *bruja* who he has business with, and the *bruja* is with one of the Yankee soldiers who burned down my village. When we arrive, he hurts Mackey so that you would open the door."

"And you just went along with him."

He went on to tell me a story I could picture vivid in my head. If he had not chosen this life of robbery and murder, I do believe Lorenzo Chavez de la Cruz could have been a storyteller of the highest order. The man possessed a gravity and a natural way of holding an audience, even small as this one was, that belied the fact he was beginning to wear his age and was tired for it. I do not imagine life as a displaced vaquero and a Mexican soldier was easy even without the introduction of George Dalton into his tale. Perhaps without George Dalton he never would have taken to robbery. Never would have taken to murder. I believed him when he told me George Dalton was older than either of us put together. Older than Mexico. Older than Europe, maybe, or maybe just the spirit riding him was. But I did believe him.

Before they picked up Kelly Mackey outside Kansas City, they rode with a band of mercenaries who had broken free from the American army and made their way through the frontier states collecting scalps, white and Indian both, and the money that came along with them. As time passed and whiskey flowed, the men began to doubt both George Dalton's story and his integrity. All the time he was with them, de la Cruz made as if he did not speak English. Dark skinned and wary eyed as he was, I doubt any of the mercenaries suspected the falseness in this.

As the story goes, one night the men had taken to drinking and in drinking rustled up enough foolish courage between the half dozen of them to draw their pistols and confront George Dalton. The men did not want to travel any farther west with a liar in their midst, they having enough lies to keep straight between the lot of them as it was, and that liar laughed though he had six guns trained on him. Told one of the men he would do just as well to put the bullet between his own eyes, and the man did so without hesitating. The rest of the men stood frozen a moment, and then they began to fire on George Dalton.

De la Cruz was not sure how many of them missed and how many of their shots rang true, but George Dalton pulled his own revolver and put a bullet into the heads and chests of the remaining five men. Had one bullet left by the time the gun swung around to aim at de la Cruz. He said, "You speak English just fine, don't you?"

And de la Cruz said to him, "*Claro.*"

And de la Cruz said to me, "I never lied to him again. I was too afraid to lie to him. After, he asks if I would not rather go back home to my family. I tell him he knows already what happened to my family, but he wants to hear me say it."

The words came out on their own. "Is my mother alive?"

"I don't know, *bruja*. She was."

"When?"

"A week ago. When we split up."

"Did he hurt her?"

"What do you think?"

"I ain't thinking. I'm asking."

"Last I saw, she was not hurt."

"Where did he take her?"

"He did not tell me where he was going."

"Bullshit," I said. "You knew my husband was a medic—"

"Un médico quien ayudó a los soldados a matar mi gente."

"He didn't kill anyone!"

"The American army," said de la Cruz, "killed my wife, my children, my mother. They take my horses and burn my land, all in the name of war. You think I do not know what it is to watch such a thing?"

"I don't care if you know!" I said. "I ain't the first person ever lost the most important thing in the world to them, and neither are you."

"Most important thing in the world is not your spouse, *chinita*, or your children. Or your land. It's your freedom, your ability to think for your own damned self. Slant-eyed *bruja* living in this godforsaken country, you of all people should know that."

I hated him then. I hated him because I agreed with him and I did not want to admit to agreeing with him. Because I do not want to pass along the words of a heartless man who spoke so free because he knew his days were not numbered in his favor.

When I stepped towards him, he did not shrink back. He stood up from his chair just as easy as you please, and he grabbed me by the wrist and spun me around so that the tip of his knife bit the skin of my neck, and, my dear, I could not help but scream. He put his forearm over my windpipe then, choked off the sound, and Roger Hawking burst in the shack door even as I was unleashing the effort I had held over Lorenzo Chavez de la Cruz as a guillotine this entire time, directing it into the handle of the knife. In seconds it grew too hot for de la Cruz to hold any longer, and he dropped it with a snarl. He seized on my momentary weakness and pushed me away from him.

I broke the fall with my hands and knees, and Hawking told him to put his damned hands in the air. He put his damned hands in the air, and the men stood staring at each other for a moment. A standoff. If I moved, it would tip the balance one way or the other, and by now you should know that I am not a gambler. Hawking was. I expected he would have recognized a stacked deck when he saw one.

"Get down on the ground!" Hawking said.

"What are you going to do?" de la Cruz asked. "Shoot me?"

"You get down on the ground and stay there till we're gone, it won't come to that."

I got to my feet and came to stand by the fireplace, as far out of the line of gunfire as I could given how little room the shack afforded us. It was not far enough to save my hearing, and Hawking was not fast enough to save himself.

As Hawking leveled the rifle and aimed, de la Cruz jumped out of the way and hid behind the table, which looked as if it had stood in that place longer than even the shack itself had. When he came up from hiding, he filled Hawking's chest with lead, six shots altogether. Hawking paused a moment, his body going into shock, then shot de la Cruz in the shoulder and fell to the floor.

Though I screamed his name and went down on my knees beside him, opened up his shirt to visualize the wounds, I knew before I even reached him that he would be dead within minutes. All six of the bullets had entered his chest, three on each side, and though the wounds themselves were bleeding, the blood was not leaving his body. He realized what I was fixing to do and shook his head, same as your father had. He grabbed my hands to keep them from doing healing work, same as your father had. It did not take long for me to make sense of the wet coughing, the air he gasped in leaving his body through the holes in his chest. He was drowning in his own blood.

My dear, I could not save him. He could not speak as he lay dying on the floor, and once I realized I could not save him, I put one hand on his forehead and took his right hand in the other and I held him. I was crying as I told him it was all right, he kept you safe, it was just going to hurt for a few more minutes, I was right there with him. Anything I could think to say to keep him from dying afraid and thinking he was alone. I felt him stop fighting as the calming spell washed over him. And then I felt his consciousness leave him. And then I felt the last of his breath go out of him. And so he left me in a shack in the middle of hell with the man who killed him.

Fear and rage will grant a body strength it might not have possessed otherwise, a numb sort of freedom in acting without thought, and my body found its strength when Hawking stopped coughing and closed his eyes and ceased to be. I grabbed the rifle from where de la Cruz had propped it by the fire, and I advanced on him. Though the table stood between us, it was not enough distance for him to evade the butt of the rifle, which I used to hit him in the throat. The blow stunned him, and I hit him again in the shoulder where Hawk had already shot him, then I hit him hard in the belly, threw down the rifle, and commenced to pummel him with my fists.

My dear, I had never in my life hit a man the way I hit the man who killed Roger Hawking. The man who was as much a liar as I had expected he would be, the man who could have been either one of us for how easy it was for the monster George Dalton to control him. I hit him with my fists, and when he regained his senses enough to grapple with me, I grabbed him by the lapels of his coat.

De la Cruz swung at me with his left hand, which I did not expect. He hit me hard in the temple, sending stars exploding across my vision. So I straddled his legs to keep him from getting away and I slammed his head on the floor. He did not stop moving. I slammed his head on the floor again.

He stopped moving, and I climbed off him, and I commenced to kicking him in the ribs, and by then I expect I was crying too hard to continue wailing on him. But I did. I wailed on him until he ceased to move, and then I kicked him one more time to assure myself he had stopped moving due to unconsciousness and not due to a ruse. I walked away from his crumpled form and sank down on the floor beside Hawking and cried though my tears served no purpose. They sure as hell were not going to bring him back to life.

That would have been the last thing he wanted, anyway.

Before I burned the shack to the ground, I took from it what items I suspected would serve some purpose on a very long journey and placed them in the satchel Hawking no longer had need for. I took Hawking's wallet and his rifle and I took de la Cruz's heavy knife, and, though I was not hungry, I ate some of the stew left hanging over the cook fire, for I had not taken a hot meal in some time and did not wish to deprive you of what you needed to grow strong.

I found another satchel on an otherwise empty chair. The contents gave me a moment's pause. Inside I found a box of ammunition, a compass stained with rusted blood, and a finger bone held intact with wire and grayed with age. While nothing in the satchel was of any immediate use, even the compass's directional markings worn away and its needle refusing to point due north, I took it anyway.

Once I had stripped the house and the corpses of what I could carry, and checked to make sure de la Cruz was no longer breathing, I walked over to the bed and looked down on Kelly Mackey. He could have been no older than thirty, and though I had only seen him in this state, broken and dragged around by men who did not care for him, I could imagine he was a religious man. I could imagine a man like George Dalton having an easy way with him. That does not mean I forgave him. I do not forgive him. I pity him, however, even now. I pity him, because if he had fought back even a little, maybe none of this ever would have happened.

Though I was quite certain he would die soon enough on his own, I held a pillow down over his face. It caused him to reach up and try to remove my hands and fall away again, dead. I left the pillow where it was and considered how I was going to burn the place to the ground.

I found I could not bring myself to burn my friend's body in the same fire as would consume de la Cruz and Mackey. So I got my hands around Hawk's cold wrists and dragged him out into the dusty air. I breathed deep and fast, letting my mind spark the flint of hatred I still carried for the liar lain out inside. What I did is considered forbidden among the women of our line, but I figured there was no coming back from where I was headed, anyway. I used the power of my thoughts to ignite the shack and give me the light I needed to gather up firewood and kindling to build a separate pyre for Hawk.

As the flames engulfed his body, I prayed to a god neither of us believed in that Hawk would find in death whatever peace had evaded him in life, and when his body was nothing but bone and ash for the wind to take, I shouldered his rifle and walked away.

I could see the shack's glow across the plains for over an hour after I had returned to the cart with two satchels and a dead man's rifle. It was not a light that offered me any warmth, and I dare say whatever warmth it offered de la Cruz was nothing compared to the fires of whatever hell awaited him.

15

THUS FAR I had spent little time thinking on what I could have done different—how I could have kept the door secured instead of letting the men in, how I could have stayed behind instead of going forward—but the reason I had done so was the uselessness of latching on to such thoughts. It is like cutting your own flesh in the hopes it will hurt someone else. There is no reason for it, yet I blame my spell of wondering that night on many things.

Fatigue and not knowing how many hundreds of miles lay between myself and the monster responsible for killing your father, the loneliness and the toll carrying you and a debt unpaid at the same time, and the weather, colder and meaner than the late autumns in St. Louis—I had plenty of bodily reasons why my mind was fixing to wander as I kept on riding, alone for the first time since George Dalton murdered your father.

If de la Cruz had known we were both there, he would have had no reason to take Hawk's appearance as a threat. If I had not lost my temper and sprung at him, if I had not screamed and alarmed Hawk, if Hawk and I had stayed in St. Louis and let the bastards go on running . . . I might have been able to let George Dalton go, if I thought Hawk were of a mind to do the same. This is what I ruminated on, and all I ended up doing was going so far back in my own history that I lived a whole other life, and that whole other life did me no good in this one.

Hawk had not jawed on much about the past while we rode together, and when he had, he had had a purpose in dredging up each particular recollection. Most of his stories were amusing, at least to him, and as I sit and think on it now I suppose he derived more pleasure from knowing I did not share his humor than he did from the humor itself. I had not had to ration our dry goods much, as the man subsisted on what to my observations appeared to be a liquid diet, but he and I had shared the burden of trapping game animals when we made our brief stops along the side of the road, and those stops would be more dangerous now. Even riding itself was a risk, as I could urge the horses on only so quickly and an unburdened rider could overtake me without difficulty.

Thinking about the past and the fanciful ways I could have changed it was a comfort compared to imagining what could befall me as I pursued the demon George Dalton, but in either case I was not focused on the road ahead, or on my environment. Being aware of my surroundings would keep me alive, and as the sun rose the morning after I killed Lorenzo Chavez de la Cruz and Kelly Mackey and burned Roger Hawking's body, I resolved to keep myself busy with what was ahead of me, and not what was behind.

In time I came to a fork in the road, one direction matching the stained compass needle and the other leading east, toward a set of roaring waterfalls. I looked down at the needle, and upon comparing it to the position of the sun in the sky saw it still did not point due north. It pointed, make no mistake, but I could not figure what it was pointing at.

I read in a book once that compasses work because the magnetic pull of the farthest end of Earth, somewhere beyond the Arctic where the ships have not yet sailed, is stronger than any other force in nature. No matter which way a body aims a compass, its needle will always swivel towards the northern pole of the planet. This one did not.

Magnets may well lose their charge, but they do not malfunction, and this compass, aside from having acquired a patina of dried blood, did not appear to have taken any damage that would account for its refusal to point north. It was then I took it for what it was—tainted by George Dalton and yearning towards him.

This may seem a hollow confession, as two men were dead on account of my pursuit of George Dalton already, three counting Roger Hawking and four counting your father, but I would let Henry Ness haul me up before Judge Crewe and I would lay my hand on a book a priest believes should burn my palm and I would attest under threat of execution that when I set out from De Soto three months earlier, my intent had been to locate and turn over to the authorities the men who had killed my husband. That was no longer my intention, as I was no longer after a man.

All the men in the tale save for Sheriff Ness were dead. I wanted George Dalton to join them, my dear, and I wanted to be the one to see certain he did.

16

THE TRAIL FROM the Badlands to the Missouri River was a stretch of terrain I would not consider a trail so much as the horses and the cart wheels' finding the clearest way and keeping to it. From time to time the compass needle would point in a direction that would have taken a single rider over steep slopes or treacherous hillsides, and we would have to go the long way around. Without Hawk there to complain about the obstacles or the biting cold, I felt more alone than I ever had in my entire life. If I were to scream, my voice would evaporate before it ever reached another human ear.

Only cold, sleepless nights passed during the hundred or so miles between the shack where three men died and the trading post on the southern bank of the Missouri. At dawn on the last day of that leg of the journey, I was heating water over a small fire to wash with when the clopping of hooves some distance away drew my attention. I looked to the west, to the trail I was leaving behind, and I saw three Sioux warriors on horseback.

They and I eyed each other for several heartbeats, assessing whether the other posed a threat. I saw three young scouts returning to their homes with news of what they had seen on the frontier, and they saw a filthy pregnant woman from an unknown tribe. Neither they nor I had any reason to confront the other. If we had, they would have found me easy to pick off.

By the time I thought to take my next breath, they had decided to keep moving. They and their horses turned away and disappeared into the copse of naked trees penning in the trail.

I was as bundled up as I could be, given we had set out from De Soto in summertime and it was now November in the northern Nebraska Territory. Soon snow would fall, and it would cover what little trail there was between myself and George Dalton. When I attempted to use my Sight to find his exact location, I could only manage a weak glimpse of his surroundings. When I attempted to apply an herbal balm to the horses' hooves, they protested my hands. This, I blamed on the unfamiliar territory and the fatigue the horses and I all felt. A month on the road is a long time for any animal, and these two were not as comfortable with me as your father's had been. It did not matter to me. What mattered was to keep moving, and so we did.

Crossing the river was an easier task than it would have been in springtime, the waterline being low as it was and crusted over with ice that the afternoon sun had not yet melted. But the compass needle had not moved, and soon I would meet the man who was responsible for all of this.

After crossing the river, I knelt by the shore to refill my canteen. My reflection peered out at me, filthy. That was nothing new. My eyes, though. They were darker, the irises no longer the ice blue of their nature. They were black. Rather than take it for warning, I ignored it and returned to the cart.

We conquered a modest hill and rounded a bend and came upon a cluster of tents. Horses ignored us, their saddles and bridles removed, their heads buried in their feed sacks. Tracks walking back and forth from the river told me the encampment had been here some time.

My first inclination when I saw the tents was to introduce myself to the men inside, to purchase supplies with money I had taken from the roadhouse. But what I saw next gave me both pause and hope.

Crosses rose up out of the frozen earth.

The men were missionaries.

Missionaries and Christians have not been caring to our kind. Our kind has always been closest to the more fundamental religions, the pagans preceding those institutions. Religions of earth and water and sky. That said, I was not planning on announcing myself as a witch, and figured I would secure nourishment for you by appealing to the charity of which I have heard many Christians speak.

Something about the crosses niggled at me, but I could not identify what it was. Voices drifted out of the large tent in the center of the encampment, behind the crosses. I reasoned it was the congregation and made my way to it.

A small stove set up at one end of the tent did little to heat the space, but the men inside, their large bodies packed in close together, must not have felt much need for it. I counted over a dozen men in the audience. Rough men, with large shoulders and unkempt beards. I wish I could tell you the man at the very front of the group, standing tall atop a makeshift stage and preaching with such terrific fervor, was the man who murdered your father. He was not.

What I am about to write is to the best of my recollection, for I felt a great yawning sensation as the realization came upon me. The compass had led me here, and if I did not step back and begin running, the demon to which it was attuned would escape again. I thought back to my mother's childhood averments, of the roles of men bearing crosses in burning our kind. Those crosses outside were not mere decoration.

They were not for praying. They had been planted upside down, to torture their victims before burning them.

As the vertigo lessened, I heard the preacher speaking of the devilry born of the heathens of the wood. Younger than I would have thought capable of commanding an audience of

weather-hardened frontiersmen, this man had a darkness in
his eyes that the men responded to. He had seen the hell of
which he spoke.

"If we descend into hatefulness, brothers, we have already
lost the battle before us. We must cooperate with God in turning what was meant for evil into a greater good within us. This
is why we bless those who would curse us: it is not only for their
sakes but to preserve our own soul from its natural response
toward hatred. It is the word of the prophet that fire will purify
these wretched devils and release their souls from the shackles
of their witchery. Since Christ has suffered in the flesh, arm
yourselves for the same purpose."

It was then that the preacher's dark eyes found me at the
back of the congregation, the only woman in the place and
filthy besides.

"My brothers!" said the preacher. "Speak of the devil, and he
will snare one of his faithful to answer for him!"

I backed out of the tent and turned to run, certain I would
be able to make it from the center of camp to the cart where
I had left the horses. I did not anticipate that the missionaries
would have such fleetness of foot, nor that two would appear
in front of me. As it was, I all but ran right into them. I used
my Will to cause one of the men to trip over his own feet and
fall to the ground, but once down he was quick to recover and
subdue me.

In spite of my scratching and shrieking, they secured my arms to my sides and dragged me over to one of the inverted crosses, which others had taken down in preparation to use it.

As the men wrestled my arms to the posts, I allowed my fury to heat the inside of my mouth, Willing it to scorch whatever it struck, and spat in the eye of one unfortunate who leaned over me. He howled as if I had hit him with a knife rather than saliva, but another took his place just as quick and put his full weight on my wrist to keep me from gaining leverage. He could not keep me from shrieking. If they had performed this act before, it would be nothing new to them. If they had not, my only hope was to unnerve them enough that they would complete the task poorly, and I would be able to escape.

One of the men was hollering above the others, encouraging them to burn me. Though I saw no signs of fire, his voice stoked the fury in my chest. Then came the voice of the preacher as he approached me, roaring the way only the righteous can.

"You have committed great sins, and I am the punishment of God, the instrument of your purification!"

I was not sure whether he was a vessel for the man who killed your father, or some form of disciple, or perhaps just a pawn whom he would soon dispatch as he had dispatched the men de la Cruz had told me of. It made no difference. The others obeyed him.

They tipped the cross back into position, hoisting my feet into the air and sending the blood rushing to my head. I saw the world upside down, my hair falling away from my scalp and coiling in the snow, the boots of the gathered men tramping about the spectacle they had made of me. To loosen the knots and free my feet and wrists ought to have been a minor bit of Work, and I did exert the effort. But the effort required clarity of mind and purity of spirit, and I could not Will the rope to loosen.

So I tried to summon the fire beneath my breast, use it to burn through the ropes. At the time, I thought I must have exhausted my resources. I must have attempted to do too much in too short a time. And I fought against the thought my magick was failing me for some other reason as much as I fought against the ropes. No matter what I spat or mumbled, the ropes remained bound fast.

I looked at my arms, seeking some sign of what was impeding my Work. Rather than iron shackles or some other difficult mechanism, I saw faint black lines running along the veins in my wrists. When I looked forward again, one of the men had returned from the fire. He crouched down before me to wave the screaming red poker in my face.

All that kept my heart beating was you, my dear. I knew what the black lines meant.

I could not see the pyre but I felt the heat and smelled the smoke.

"Not yet, not yet!" The preacher's voice was thunder rolling over the landscape. "Our father is not yet with us! She cannot burn yet!"

I looked at the empty crosses to my left and right, waiting for Dalton to appear. Waiting for them to string your gran up next to me.

This was how I feared our story would end. Dalton would come to witness his handiwork. He would bring what was left of your gran with him, and he would rip you from my belly and pin you to your own cross, and we would all burn together on these rough beams tied into a shape men long ago convinced themselves was holy.

What happened next I neither expected nor witnessed. It was the retort of the rifle that I heard, a bare moment before the head of the man who had been holding the branding iron sprayed blood and brain onto the snow in front of me.

More shots rang out. The owner of the rifle was calm, his shots deliberate. I heard horses setting off as I fought to stay conscious, heard the preacher shouting in vain to keep his congregation from dispersing. The sound of a rifle stock firmly connecting with a skull ended his preaching.

The smoke was thick and I could barely see. A figure paced toward me and I listened to his footfalls, saw his boots before I saw the rest of him. The figure knelt down next to me.

"Hello, Lilian," said Sheriff Henry Ness.

17

AS THE SHERIFF could no more put me on the back of his horse than he could bear to have me walk along of him in the frigid cold with his friend's child growing in my belly, he loaded me into the back of my own cart. He lashed his horse to it as well, climbing up into the driver's seat where the butcher and I had passed so many months together and leaving me in the back, beneath blankets and among my dwindling supplies.

This was not how I had envisioned my journey ending, and I was not of a mind to allow it to end this way, but Ness shackled my feet as well as my wrists. I could no more entertain ideas of running than I could entertain ideas of rescue. I was too weak to cast a spell to break the mechanisms keeping the shackles closed, or cast a hex to set the sheriff's brains to boiling. For the moment, I was his prisoner, and though I could no longer see the compass needle pointing the way, I knew in my gut Dalton was not far from us. I do not know how to explain my intuition, and I hope this is nothing you ever learn to recognize. He was near. I know this much.

Ness drove the cart through what was left of the day and into the dusk, stopping only when continuing would have proven too dangerous. Once stopped, he went about setting up camp, building a fire and tending to the horses and dragging me out of the back of the cart to secure me by the warmth of the flames. Though I asked where his deputy was, Ness was not interested in talking until he had cooked supper and sat down by the fire himself.

Were I alone, I might have refused food to prove a point. But I was unable to make use of Eva's protective herbs while under arrest, and you needed nourishment more than anything else. So I ate and waited for Ness to speak.

"Where's Hawking?" he asked.

"Dead," I said.

"How?"

"The Mexican shot him."

"Where's the Mexican?"

"Dead. I beat him to death after he shot Hawk. Then I smothered the Irishman."

"Jesus, Lilian." I thought that would be the end of the conversation, but he went on, "You're a goddamned fool. You're with child. Those men nearly killed you."

"What do you care?" I asked. "You were going to hang me."

Ness came over and undid the irons on my hands and feet.

"What are you doing?"

He removed a mass of paper from his pocket and unfolded it before laying it in front of me. I flinched when recognition hit me. He had found the page George Dalton had planted in Aunt Griselda's mouth.

"I believe you," Ness said.

"Where did you get that?" I asked.

"I went to St. Louis to wait for you. Three men matching the description you gave in De Soto arrived just before you did. A Mexican who gave his name as Lorenzo Chavez de la Cruz, an Irishman mad with gangrene, and a blond man dressed in black. I lost track of them, but I figured if I followed you, you would lead me to them. I lost you in the Badlands and picked you up a day back. Now, you've got every reason in the world to hate me, and I won't begrudge you that, but the way I see it, we need each other if we're going to see the man who killed Matt hang for what he did."

As I looked at him, I saw the toll the last few months had taken on Ness. Behind his scraggly beard were sunken cheeks and a haunted gaze. Figuring I had nothing left to lose, I decided to trust him.

"He ain't a man, Hank. I don't know what he is, but whatever he is ain't of this world. The Mexican says he's older than this country, and I found a compass in his hide-out that don't point north."

Ness asked, "You expect me to believe George Dalton is some kind of . . . what, devil?"

"Not the way you mean it. But he ain't a man, neither. Whatever he is, he's powerful. It'll take more than a six-shooter to bring him in."

Though Ness was not exactly picking up what I was putting down, neither did he appear to think I had lost what was left of my mind.

"I seen all manner of Indians called themselves shamans," Ness said, "and down Mexico way I seen holy men who thought they came from gods. They all bled just the same as me."

There is more sense in arguing with a wall than there is in arguing with a man, but I wonder now that I know the ending of the story if I ought not have argued with him harder. If my hands will feel clean after all that they have done, if my eyes will ever shine blue again, or if I will walk the earth with black eyes and veins, the mark of devilry in me not from chance but from my own damned choices.

I do not know what Henry Ness thought he was chasing. But when I awoke the next morning, he was gone, as was the compass.

18

NESS HAD LEFT me supplies and horses. I imagined in his
way he was trying to keep me safe. Absent the compass, I had
no means to track Dalton. And you were coming soon. I stuck
between the forest and the river, scanning for any sign of Ness,
or Dalton, or my mother. If Ness did not find me, I figured,
Dalton would sooner or later.

On the third day, I started finding body parts scattered
along the path. Late in the morning I found a foot, still in its
boot, along the side of the path I was following. An hour or so
later, I found an ear. It was resting atop a snowdrift, as if set in
the most visible place possible, and dread began to overtake my
hunger. They were like mile markers from a Christian's notion
of hell, and the higher the sun rose the less at ease I felt, and
from time to time I heard the cawing of crows. Each time, I
inspected the discarded appendage closely, fearing it belonged
to either Ness or my mother. By the time the sun had swung

around the meridian and was heading towards the horizon, I had found a hand, blue and dappled with ice crystals. It wore no jewelry, and its size suggested it had belonged to a man.

Eventually I had to stop and make camp. On a normal night I would have extinguished the fire before turning in, not wanting to risk its burning out of control or giving away my location, but the horses were as uneasy as I was, and besides, in ten hours of riding we had seen no sign of the head belonging to the rest of the pieces. I had trouble sleeping knowing it was still out there somewhere, and as soon as the sky was gray enough to see by the next morning, I broke camp and got back on the road.

On the fourth day, when I was now well north of anything that could pass for signs of civilization, my eyes had just about gone to sleep from the sameness of the landscape when a neglected signpost flashed red at me. The horses slowed without my clucking to them, and the source of the red tightened my jaws.

The body had neither skin nor scalp. By the slimness in the hips and the broadness of the chest, I could tell it was a man's. It had not been there long enough to freeze solid, but he had been dead long enough for scavengers to have had at him. In the center of its chest, a metal badge had been stabbed through the bone. It did not pull away from the body as the gory mess turned over to reveal its decoration to me.

I consider myself a woman of strong constitution and character, but I had to steady myself on the side of the cart and vomit.

If the body, or what was left of the body, belonged to Henry Ness, I did not want to know. I had my suspicions, and I still have my doubts. That body could have belonged to anyone, as could the badge. Coincidences abound in the wild, yet I cannot lie and tell you that I would have felt anything if the body had turned out to be the sheriff's. I was beyond grief, then. All I had room for was anger.

After I had been on the desolate road for a week and a half, I began to fear I would not see another settlement before my food stores began to run out. All around me were trees and snow, but a body cannot subsist off bark and water. My body was not my own. My belly grew bigger, yet my stomach growled from the time I rose in the morning until the time night fell not even eight hours later.

On the tenth day, the horses and I found ourselves walking into a relentless wind, with gusts that brought tears to my eyes and forced me to tie my scarf in such a fashion that I could breathe but not see. I had to trust the horses and my own sense of direction.

In time the wind began to bring with it a scent I thought certain to be a product of my imagination. Were it not for the fact that the horses reacted to it before I did, that they made high distressed noises and balked when I flicked their reins, I might have considered ignoring it. Might have, but for the fact that I was not smelling rabbit or duck or even a larger game animal, boar or bear or elk.

I allowed the horses to stay where they were while I climbed down from the cart. Putting my back to the wind took away some of its sting, and I unwrapped my face that I would have full use of my senses, if only for a moment. It was then I heard the crackling of the fire, and was able to follow it farther off the path. Another crackle, this time beneath my boot. I had stepped not on a downed branch, but a rib picked clean of meat. I found another a few feet away. In another few feet, I reached a small clearing.

Someone had left a thick hunk of meat, flayed and skewered by the bone, roasting over a fire. My stomach growled and cramped at once, my hunger at war with the horror I felt, the uncertainty.

Perhaps it was not human flesh, after all. If it was, it may well have been your gran's. At least, this is what I reminded myself as I considered what I had stumbled upon. That I had stumbled upon it meant someone had left it there for me. Mocking me.

I stood in the clearing a while longer, daring the demon whose presence I could not feel to show himself, and when he did not, I spat to clear my mouth of water and returned to the cart.

On the eleventh day, I stopped for a meager lunch scraped together from what was left of my stores, and in doing so I realized I had run clean out of the tea Eva had blessed to keep you where you were. I rummaged through all of the bags and sacks in the cart, but I had no luck in finding any pouches or stray dry leaves that I could use to barter another day or two of travel without worrying about your coming early. I had loved you since the moment of your quickening, but this was not the place where I wanted to bring you into the world, nor was it the time.

I rode the horses another ten miles or so after that, stopping when I realized I needed to hunt for meat in addition to setting up camp for the night. That time of year is miserable for hunting, and so close to the end of my pregnancy as I was, I could hardly sneak through the woods with its dead leaves and frozen underbrush and pursue what creatures were still foraging for food without giving myself away, but I found myself lucky. As dusk fell I came upon a doe limping through the forest with a miscarried foal, still in its sac, trailing frozen behind her. She was weak and unsteady on her feet, and I would like to think shooting her was a kindness nature would not have afforded her had I not come along. Her pelt was mangy and her meat stringy, but I made use of what I could and left the rest for the scavengers.

That night, the wind howled, and though the horses nestled together under their thick blankets I knew they were cold and restless. I hardly slept myself. My ears confused the howls of the wind with the screaming of the victims I imagined the demon George Dalton to be skinning in the darkness. On more than one occasion, I awakened thinking I had heard my mother's voice.

It was to be the last night of true rest, and I let nightmares pick away at it until I rose in the morning raw-boned and frozen, my back aching something fierce. The way the sun rose, its color or its fierceness or maybe just my own imagination, told me today was the day I was going to find the demon. Whatever it was, it was right.

Later that morning I surmised the demon George Dalton had come upon a group of prospectors out in the woods the night before, and this group of prospectors had taken a shine to him.

I could imagine him sitting around the fire with them, brewing coffee and telling jokes, his eyes just as dead and cold as the land around them, looking at all of them like they were nothing while they thought to themselves that they had had themselves a spell of good luck running into another pair of hands and a man willing to work for his supper, prospecting being miserable business this time of year but profitable if you could survive the cold. And I did imagine him. As I did not encounter him at this campsite, I could do nothing more than imagine him.

And as I rode, I found imagining him gave me something to focus on other than the discomfort in my back and belly. I refused to believe it was you getting ready to come into the world. I wanted to believe you would stay put until I had strung the demon up, or at least secured him to the horse and started dragging him on back to Fort Pierre, where I would tell the prospectors what they really had in their midst. I would say, *Look, look at this snake. You all let him just slide on through here after he killed five people between here and the southern territory, after he killed my husband and the father of my child.* I could not even tell them how many were dead in Louisiana because of him. *A lawman's pieces lie scattered between here and the Missouri River, with no accounting for his head. Your lord only knows how many more dead lie so in his shadow. Look.*

And I imagined the night your father died, because I wanted to have that fire hot in my breast when I finally caught up with Dalton. I imagined that feeling of holding my breath, warning Hawk to be careful, just before the ground fell out from under me, before George Dalton shot your father and shot Hawk and took my mother.

As the horse and I rode along the coastline, we began to find bodies again. Unlike the bodies on the road, these bodies were bobbing in the slushy surf in the lake, the waves rolling in white capped and angry, the first of the bodies full clothed and facedown, and I thought it must have been an accident. But then as we kept riding and we got closer to the next campsite,

I started feeling like I felt that night George Dalton shot your father, this faint feeling like someone was grabbing me by the back of the neck and holding me over open air, and we rode past another body. And another. And another. And I began to imagine, because it was imprinted in the landscape of the place and I was attuned to it, I knew more then than I had known before, that the demon George Dalton had suspected they were beginning to learn too much, or they were getting too friendly, or he had felt my presence in the settlement, and he had compelled the men one at a time to stand up from their morning necessaries and walk into the lake far enough that when they drowned the only thing that would get them back to shore was the surf catching their dead weight and carrying it the rest of the way.

Eight bodies we passed, all told. Not even the birds chirped. Nothing but the sound of the water lapping at the stones and the sand, but the horse's hooves stamping through the snow. That dead silence kept after us for miles as I urged the old girl on faster. I was more weight than she was used to carrying on her back, and she had not had a night's rest since Hawk died. In spite of her lather and her buckling knees, I urged her on.

It came as no surprise to me that the horse could run only so fast for so far, and yet I allowed myself to feel frustration and anger as she gave a final wheezing whinny and collapsed into the snow, unable to get up again. I climbed out of the saddle, and she fell over onto her side, dead.

The galloping had been hard on my hips, but it was not the hours of riding so hard that had taken away my breath. It was not long before I realized what was happening. You were coming whether I wanted you to or not. I continued on foot, fast as I could with the band of pain tightening and releasing faster than it had before.

The sky was dark and the full moon bright overhead when I reached the apex of a final hilltop and the salt-rimmed lakeshore revealed itself, and the figures before it.

One of the figures was bound to a stake planted in the lake's shallow shores. Steam rose from the lake's surface like spectral witnesses to the coming atrocity. The figure was my mother. Your grandmother, Catriona MacPherson.

Ministering to the stake was the other figure, the tall black-clad hunter known as George Dalton. He had his back to me, though I had no doubt in my mind he was aware of my presence, and I could not hear what he said as he grabbed hold of the top of the stake and tugged, easy as unearthing a blade of grass. The stake fell into the icy sludge that winter had made of the water, and it swallowed my mother up.

I had started running before the stake had even tipped—at least, as fast as I was able to run with a full-grown baby ready to leave my belly—while screaming for my mother.

Dalton stood aside, making no effort to stop me from plunging into the water after your gran. The cold grabbed hold of my knees and nearly pulled me down, all the muscles responsible for keeping me upright flaring with a sensation I mistook for heat, so unlike any cold I had ever felt before as it was. In the wake of the pain from the freezing water came another band of pain, this one so intense I nearly went down on my hands and knees in the lake. Had I, we all would have drowned out there. I braced myself on my knees, cursing myself for my weakness in that moment, and when it passed, I gathered up my strength and grabbed hold of the stake, my gloved hands shaking with a fierceness I could not control.

Once we were back on the rocky shore, I crouched and began to work at the ropes binding my mother's body to the stake. My fingers were stiff and numb, refusing to do as I pushed them to do, and I was shivering so hard I could not get a good grip on the waterlogged rope. I was beginning to consider using a knife to cut her free when that band tightened in my belly again.

It was then I felt a pain so hot and bloody that I screamed for the first time since the pains had started, sending me to my hands and knees with nothing but Hawking's rifle slung across my back for either protection or companionship.

When I first felt you quickening in the springtime, I thought I would give birth to you in front of the fireplace at home. I had watched my aunts give birth to my younger cousins, and I had helped deliver more than a few of De Soto's new babies. Helping deliver a baby is a different matter than giving birth yourself.

The fire spreading to the center of my body told me there would be no more willing you to stay where you were. I could only get my trousers down around my knees, but that was far enough to do what I needed to do. Still on my hands and knees, I pushed. Then I fell onto my back in the snow. The blood and the fluid from the sac soaked the earth underneath me, and I had only enough time to catch my breath before I had to push again. So I pushed and I could not help but scream that time.

My sweet, longed-for child, there you were at last, and the only thought I had as the blackness closed in around me was to let you lie in my trousers because they were warm and dry and I was not thinking straight at all by then.

I was bleeding more than I had ever seen a woman bleed before. It seemed even my eyes were covered in blood as everything went very dark. The last thing I remember is reaching for you as I heard footsteps crunching in the snow, coming towards us.

19

BEFORE I TELL YOU what he told me, I want to give you the story of your kinswoman who burned at the stake for what she did in Scotland.

Your gran's mother, my Nana Sorcha, her great-grandmother was named Eimhir. Eimhir, like many of the women of the MacPherson clan, loved a man who had to answer for his love, and rather than staying in town to risk their neighbors turning them in, they built their own home in the woods, and according to the story passed down through the generations, Eimhir bore her man two children. The firstborn, Sorcha, survived, while the son perished, as many children perished in those days. Though their hearts ached, Eimhir and her man held out hope for the day she would bear a third, for the number three carries much luck and good fortune in the Work of women with Celtic blood. Though Eimhir Worked all the fertility spells she could think of, though her family blessed a circle around her and she and her man loved each other very much, they had no success in conceiving a third child before Eimhir's man was run down in the street, either by highwaymen or townspeople who believed him to be enthralled by a witch.

If Eimhir had gone mad, this would make the tale easier to understand. Grief causes all manner of turmoil in the hearts and minds of those left behind, and though Eimhir had her sisters to support her, and though her kin Worked all of the magick in their books to turn the tides in her favor again, Eimhir did not trust that the goodness of their magick was enough to overcome the greed of Death, and so she stole away into the woods sometime after her man's burial. She toppled the caern placed over his grave, and she dug through the dirt with her own nails, and she dragged him back to the house they had built for their children and there she enacted magick so dark it has been recorded, sure, but those who recorded it would never speak of it.

Death is a natural part of living, but it is the end of life as well. Just as healing is a natural process, so is dying. All that you can do for a dying person is help them in their passage to the other side, ease their suffering that they may let go and leave behind an empty shell, rather than allow themselves to be fettered to objects or places or, worst of all, people who cause them to become *tash*. Ghosts.

There is nothing to be done for one who has ceased to live and has since become a body. Not unless you are willing to give up your own soul and become a shell that you might barter with the spirits on the other side. This is the darkness of the magick I considered after your father died, but my wits returned to me, and I convinced myself that your father deserved peace.

Necromancy is a forbidden practice, and for good reason. Your ancestor Eimhir bargained with spirits she did not understand, and she invited one into her dead man's body, and when he rose again he did so with a thirst for blood. Somehow, the story goes, Eimhir did become pregnant by what had made a home out of her dead man's body. When the witch hunters came to town and sent her man back to the earth to which he belonged and strung her up to burn for the sin she had committed, even her kin had no interest in trying to save her. That story marked the MacPherson women's slow escape from Scotland. We all know it, and now you do as well.

Prior to reading the page I pulled from Aunt Griselda's mouth, I did not know the history the witch hunters had with our family. What I know now has tainted the story as I knew it. As I knew it, Eimhir's was a cautionary tale, a warning meant to steer my cousins and me away from blacker magick. I do not believe Eimhir caused the grief of which George Dalton convicted her, but neither do I believe he killed her for committing necromancy. Your gran can tell you the story as she knows it, knowing as she will what became of the fiend who burned her great-great-grandmother.

20

WHEN I AWAKENED, I felt warm. Not so far away, Matthew was preparing dinner. I tugged at the blanket covering me, but it was only the frozen collar of my overcoat. My eyes were frozen shut, and I fought them open.

Above me, the black sky stretched out cold and vast, the constellations brighter than the snow beneath. My legs were exposed, but I felt nothing. The ground between my thighs had glutted itself on my blood. Last I had known, you were still attached to me. I reached down and found you gone.

Your gran's body lay beside me still, no longer bound to the stake. Someone had crossed her wrists over her heart. Her face was strong and calm, even in the absence of breath. Before I could tend to the dead, I had to tend to the living.

I scanned the shoreline for the source of the footsteps I had heard before I lost consciousness. Some forty paces down the shore, the flames of a small fire whispered to each other. By the firelight was a stout log, a throne for the silhouette of a tall, dark figure. At his hip was a hatchet, its blade deep in the log, in his arms a tiny bundle. You were in the arms of the demon George Dalton.

I found my feet fast, and dropped to my hands and knees faster. Between my loins and my soles, the flesh was without sensation. I whispered an incantation to revive them, and repeated it faster when it did not take. I kneaded my muscles, coaxing the blood now racing through my veins to return to my legs. It was a fruitless effort, and one that both confounded and frightened me.

So you became my beacon as I began to crawl towards the fire, the frozen earth clawing at my empty belly. In the time consumed by the last stretch of unforgiving ground, I took my first good look at the monster holding you. He had a broad face, with high, weather-worn cheekbones and deep-set eyes, black and pitiless as the bottom of a well. I recognized the pitched crown of his wide-brimmed hat.

I crouched beside the fire pit like a wounded animal and waited for the fire to thaw my useless limbs. Even wounded animals still have their teeth. I fought for a first glimpse of you, to see that you were alive, but you were nestled deep in his arms and he had no intention of giving you back to me.

"Congratulations, witch," he said. "It's a girl." He spoke in a decayed English accent, something from long ago, from tomes in the Library. "You know, hunters once believed that a witch, having rejected her baptism, would float upon being thrown into water. It was known as the cold-water test." His eyes flicked over in the distance from where I had come. "Your poor mother sank like a stone."

I would not cry. I would not give him the satisfaction of watching me cry. He removed a canteen from beneath his overcoat, and though you started to cry then, I was relieved to know your lungs were strong enough for crying. As he tipped a drop of water from the canteen onto your forehead, he began to whisper.

"I baptize you with water for repentance, but he who is coming after me is mightier than I, whose sandals I am not worthy to carry." His voice had turned singsong. "He will baptize you with the Holy Spirit and fire."

The demon was baptizing you.

"Matthew, three-eleven," he went on, turning towards me. "I don't know about the sandals, but the fire is appropriate."

"Only one of us is going in that fire," I said.

"She has your eyes, Li Lian. Had, anyway." He laughed. "You're welcome, by the way. But we'll get to that."

Until my limbs were thawed, I needed him to keep talking. So long as he was talking, you were safe.

So I asked him, "Why are you doing this?"

"I was a priest, you know." The demon traced an inverted cross on your brow as he spoke. "The Church brought us together, soldiers turned priests turned soldier-priests. Each of us, so perfectly devoted to Christ, to our Church. They sent us to root out the devils in our midst set against our Redeemer. And we did. I drowned and burned my way through the borderlands and all of Scotland."

"You killed innocent women," I said.

"Innocence." He cackled. I tried to rise to my feet but collapsed. "I let the others prick and drown and burn the silly girls who would chant whatever nonsense for nourishment. While they tortured, I traveled. I studied. Do you know what I found? Knowledge, Li Lian, older than my Church. It was in the hills of Spain, above Zugarramurdi, where I experienced a revelation. We were standing at the mouth of a cave called Infernuko Erreka by the local people. An inquisitor had tied children to a stake there. He asked me to count the children. I counted twelve."

"If there's a point to your babble, I can't conjure it."

Months on the road with Hawk had afforded me ample time to practice deflection by means of sarcasm. Dalton grinned, and despite the soullessness in his expression, I have to say the shadows suited him. Wooed him, even.

"One of the girls, she was no more than fourteen, and she stared back at me. I had never met such resoluteness, such defiance. That it should come from a young girl only impressed me all the more. I could not hear what she said, but she whispered, and the other children stopped crying all at once, even as the flames engulfed them. None of them screamed. I remarked upon this to my guide, who told me to watch closely. When the fire was extinguished, he wanted to know what I saw. I told him I had seen a great purification take place. 'No, no,' he said, 'look closer.' Upon observing the burnt remains, I finally understood then what my guide had wanted me to see. Eleven bodies, where my eyes had counted twelve."

"If your plan is to kill me with stories about faulty arithmetic," I said, "I will kindly take my child and go."

Dalton laughed before he went on, "My guide had seen this before, in a different mass purification, with the same defiant girl. She was impervious to fire. My guide believed she allowed herself to be taken to the stake that she might cast a spell over the other children, to keep them from feeling any pain. He considered this act of defiance a sin above all others, for how would the children be purified if they felt no pain? It is the pain you feel, the pain of burning and drowning, that saves you. That witch had damned their souls to hell for eternity, just as the devil wanted."

"The devil told you that?"

"He did, Li Lian."

"And what'd you have to say about that?"

"Funny you should ask. My guide asked me this very question. He wished to know what I thought about the matter, and I'll tell you what I told him: this was the first instance of true magick I had ever witnessed. In fact, it confirmed the suspicion I had held ever since I left Scotland and set out alone."

"That you didn't know the first thing about witches?"

He laughed again. The sound turned my stomach. "That witchcraft was a rare affliction rather than a skill one could acquire through compact with the devil. I recalled to my guide my own interrogations, the conflicting testimonies, the hysterias. After much wine and argument, he agreed that they were but silly girls or disturbed men. Yes, they had sought a pact with the devil. Yes, they were enemies of the Church. But no, they did not have magick. No, they were not witches. It wasn't in their blood. Not like the girl in Spain. Not like you, Li Lian. You are a true witch. Not so easy to kill, or to burn. Not without help from something equally powerful. So I ask you the same question I asked the inquisitor: How does a mortal man combat such powers?" He continued without awaiting my answer. This was his stage, and he was enjoying his performance. "That question was answered. But not by my guide, or by my God."

"Ain't no God," I said. "Not the way your book tells it."

"You may be right," he said. His eyes burned into me. "But there certainly is a devil."

He came to stand so close to the fire that the sparks jumped onto his coat.

"So you came after me and Matthew, my mother and her sisters, because you ain't found no other calling in two hundred years besides hunting witches?"

"Calling?" Dalton asked. "Is that what you think this is?" Laughter made his voice sing like a fresh-honed blade. "Maybe in the beginning. But I hunt your kind now for the same reason you hunted me."

"I wasn't hunting you for sport," I said.

"You believe, because you've done nothing to me, that this makes you innocent? Li Lian, I dare say you are about as innocent as your dead hag of a mother."

"You're the one killing innocent people. Your book don't allow that, last I heard."

"Oh, but He does. By omission, God allows all manner of evil in this world." He cast his gaze into the heart of the fire. "A child. A wife. A home. I had those things too, once. The Church would not have approved of them. I kept them to myself."

I let him wander through his memories, but I watched you in his arms. My body ached to hold you, to glimpse your face. I opened and closed my fingers, and they remembered what it was to move. I thought of de la Cruz's knife secreted in my boot. It would not kill him, but I might be able to wrest you from him.

"And then I lost them," Dalton said. "It began with a cough. No, not quite a cough. My little girl was choking. I found tiny animal bones in her bile, entangled by herbs that grow only in the Highlands of Scotland. And then came the fever. Sweat blistered her forehead. She lay shaking in my arms during the day, her eyes pleading for help, but there was nothing I could do. And when night fell, she would howl in our bed as though she were burning alive." He paused, his eyes closed in foul pantomime of a man lost in his own memories. "She died on a

Sunday. My wife blamed me, my work. She believed witches had cursed our family. She held on to that blame, and her Bible, until the same death as claimed our child came for her. In the span of a fortnight, Li Lian, I found myself utterly alone. Just as you are now alone. But I didn't blame myself, or God." He turned away from the fire to look at me. "I blamed you."

So soon as I opened my mouth, he held up a hand. He moved you closer to the flame, demonstration of where my protests would cast you.

"Of course you weren't born yet. But the seed of your lineage had already begun to sprout roots. I swore that so long as I held breath in my lungs, I would rid the earth of your kind. And that's when my prayers were answered."

I asked, "Why is it every time a madman's prayers are answered, a witch burns?"

"I prayed, Li Lian. I prayed, and I studied, and I searched. And I found she who had taken my family. Your great-great-great-grandmother Eimhir. She was hiding in Horse Meadow—Marc Innis, in your people's tongue. Of course the old crone denied what she had done, they always do, but after I peeled away a few layers of her skin, she became much more cooperative." He adopted a mocking, high-pitched brogue. "'I'll confess, I'll confess, just make it stop.'" He ceased his mimicry. "Unlike Eimhir, I cannot say I held up my end of the bargain." He waited for my response and I gave him none. "Have you heard this story before?" he asked. "Surely you have. Eimhir, granddaughter of Mór, the witch's daughter who ran off with the parson's son, your line's namesake? Your ancestor?"

I stared at him, my face wrenched in anger but silent.

"No?" He feigned injury. "I thought you'd have heard about that one. I husk an old woman, and nobody in your family talks about it? It hurts to be forgotten."

"All the pain you've inflicted," I said, "all the women you've killed, you'll have to excuse me if I can't scrounge up a damn to give you."

I thought I knew what it was to feel cold, until I looked him right in the eye as he smirked at me.

"Killing one of you was hardly a drop in the ocean, and I realized I would have to make my own sacrifice if I hoped to drain it. I prayed, not to my God but to the world beyond ours, the world from which you draw your power. And that world sent answer to my prayers."

I could not tell where the man ended and the spirit began. Neither could he, I imagine. Dalton went on: How he had followed us. To Salem. Across the Americas to our south. How he killed us wherever he found us. How all this work had brought us here, to this moment. To me. The witch-turned-huntress. Did I not appreciate how our positions were reversed?

"Don't lament," he said. "You weren't the first to hunt me and fail. After I scattered your family, the bishops accused me of witchcraft. They believed I had fallen from priesthood to devilry. My methods had become too much for them. But I did not flee. I let them come to me, and I purified them as well."

You stirred in your swaddle, opened your eyes, and began to cry again. A yearning I had never known before brought tears to my eyes.

"Ah, there, there," he cooed, rocking you in his arms above the flames. "Soon, none of this will matter, little girl."

"If you're going to kill me," I said, "quit your yapping, and get on with it."

"Anyone can kill," Dalton said, "or set fire to flesh. Flesh does not interest me. To truly purify the soul of a witch, one must turn her spirit to ash. Do you see the difference? One must diminish a witch to her barest and lowest quality. For you, that's vengeance. That is what I have done for you, Li Lian. That is why your magick is failing you. That is my gift to you. Your suffering will be your purification."

"And what's your barest and lowest quality, demon?"

A boyish grin flickered across his face as he considered me, cocking his head.

"You want to hurt me, don't you?" he asked. I neither saw the point in lying nor felt I owed him the truth. "You've allowed your soul to become consumed by revenge, the greatest fire there is, and you've nearly attained purity. If this is what you truly desire, then there is only one final thing left to do."

He strode to the opposite side of the fire. Tears streamed down my face as he held you over the blaze. I found my balance and readied myself to leap in after you. I would cover your body with mine and shield you the way a fallen tree protects the flowers during a forest fire. If he thought I would just lie still and let him burn my baby right in front of me, then I do not believe George Dalton knew me near as well as he believed he did.

When he released you, I reached out my hands and gasped a spell that would part the flames so that they would not touch you. Not knowing if the spell had taken, not trusting it after my Work had failed me so many times in such recent memory, I jumped into the fire after you. It gnawed at my legs and feet, but it could not blister the skin. From the white-hot coals I scooped you up and clasped you to my breast.

Tears have a cleansing power of their own, under certain conditions. This was a condition I could not have met before I met you. You changed me, my dear. I held you in my arms for the first time, and you made a mother out of me.

Dalton recoiled not from the fire, but from me. At the time, I thought nothing of it, but I know now he had expected to have broken me by the time he released you. That I would have nothing left to fight with. That I would be the one to burn.

I stirred the embers from within the fire and, as I had the night I burned de la Cruz and Mackey in their cabin, I bid the fire roar up hotter and higher than it could have on its own. The flames reached out and coiled around Dalton's ankles and wrists.

As the flame engulfed him, Dalton began to pray in a dead language and raised his arms again. I felt his mind reach out to mine, the malevolent entity inside him now willing me to release him as it had willed those men to walk into the lake.

I held you tight and fought for my sense, but the spirit brought me to my knees. A disembodied voice whispered to me, bid me cast you back into the fire myself. Though I could no longer hold Dalton at bay, I clutched you, somehow noiseless in all of this, to my breast.

Dalton paced towards me, rubbing at his wrists as if they were sore from handcuffs and clicking his tongue in disapproval. He reeked of burning flesh.

"I see your purification is still incomplete, Li Lian."

I murmured a protection spell beneath my breath and struggled to find my feet again, to turn and run from him. But the spirit rooted me in place. Dalton was mere paces from us now, his arms extended to take you from me.

"Come, come," the demon said in a soothing voice, "let me take her."

My grasp began to fail not because the cold had claimed my strength, but because a force beyond my control was prying my fingers from you. I pled aloud, as if my tears and my voice could do what my Will could not, but each time the word *please* passed my lips, another finger abandoned me. By the time the demon's shadow fell over us, all that kept you from tumbling to the ground was the crook of my arm and my smallest, weakest finger.

I searched his eyes to separate the man from the demon, unable to distinguish the two, and then they went wide. As I watched, something came plunging through him, driving him forward.

It was a wooden stake, now slick with his innards.

He coughed, spraying us with blood I did not flinch away from. His hands dropped down from the sky and hung at his sides a moment. Before I could breathe relief, he reached to grab the bloodied point, trying to push it out of him as if it were no more a nuisance than a splinter in the pad of his smallest finger.

But the stake drove farther through him, drove him to his knees.

It was not the spirit's releasing me that caused me to gasp.

Your gran's hair was frozen into gray-red ringlets, her skin pale as the waters that had nearly claimed her. She stood behind him, her ragged breath steaming as it left her body, and said nothing before releasing the cross to which Dalton had bound her. He fell backwards, the stake end ripping through him until his back came to rest on the cross bar.

I tightened the arm supporting you and used my free hand to move aside the fabric covering your face. You were content in your swaddle, your cheeks pink and your eyes closed, though when I brushed my fingers across your face, you blinked and tried to move your bound arms. This was the first time I laid eyes on you, and all of the pain and fear that had driven me so far melted away to reveal something stronger.

After a moment to accept your gran's assistance in strapping you to my bare chest and tucking you away under my coat again, I was ready. We set about our next task without conference. Your gran retrieved a length of rope the demon had packed away in his mare's saddlebag while I stood and kept eyes on our prisoner.

Dalton was not dead. He tried to chant, or curse, but his lung was pierced, and the only sound he was capable of producing was a bloody gurgle.

You will not remember this, but you were there. We lashed him to his own cross. Though he had no air, he was still alive, his eyes raging. And with the remaining rope, we hoisted him over the high limb of the tree above the fire from which he had sought to roast us. Your gran and I called the flames to him, and they took root. The only noise then was the crackle of his flesh.

I wanted him to watch me watch him die. His eyes were open, staring down at me. As he writhed, I removed from my boot the knife I had taken from de la Cruz, and I was a moment away from plunging it into his chest when the flickering of fire on metal caught my eye.

Without thought or hesitation, I dropped the knife into the snow, ripped the hatchet from its resting place, and took George Dalton's head. It felt to me the only way to sever the tie that had bound his line and ours for over two hundred years. It was not the first time I proved myself wrong.

By the time I realized what I had done, I was taking a hard step back, gasping from the impact of something unholy colliding with my breastbone and tunneling beneath it. It made itself right at home.

Memories that did not belong to me pushed aside my own. I saw cloistered men in the catacombs of old churches. I saw the rolling plains of our homeland. And I saw young girls roasting like pigs on cross-like spits, their screams echoing in my mind and throughout my frame. I would have collapsed beneath the weight of it if my body were my own. But it was not. It is not.

The spirit used my body to breathe in deep, and the smell of Death hanging in the air pleased me.

I looked at Dalton's corpse for the last time, his white teeth gleaming in his charred face. Smiling at me. You began to cry again, the longing in your voice drawing me back to the duty that would force me to leave you.

Your gran asked me what happened.

She called my name, her voice trailing off as I approached Dalton's white mare, still tied to the burning tree.

The horse reared in the orange glow, flinching at my outstretched hand. My voice Worked to soothe her alarm. I untied her reins and stroked her neck and helped your gran into the saddle. She set her steely-blue eyes on me, but did not ask again what I had seen after killing Dalton.

It was just you and me and your gran then, a hundred miles from the nearest human settlement and with a journey through deep snow and frigid winds ahead of us. But the sun was rising and I did not despair. I slung Hawk's rifle across my back and began to walk.

Ninety miles we traveled from the bloodstained shores of the lake of the spirits to Davenport, Iowa, where we secured passage downriver to St. Louis. It is from a cabin on the riverboat that I watch you sleep and finish writing this letter to you. I awakened early this morning to find myself on the bow of the boat, holding your swaddled form over the vessel's churning wake. The spirit that was in George Dalton is ancient and insatiable, and I am afraid of what has taken root in me. More and more each day, there is less and less of me.

When we disembark, your gran will take you to the roadhouse, where she will raise you up, safe, and you will see me again when I have learned how to banish this spirit that has made its way into my bones.

Your name is Sarah Callahan, and you come from a line of women gifted in a way that scares most folks, and I will let nothing harm you.

LIST OF PATRONS

Adam Gomolin
Ben Luntz
Billy O'Keefe
Jonna M. Terhune
Larry Levitsky
Thad Woodman
Thomas J. Arnold

INKSHARES

INKSHARES is a reader-driven publisher and producer based in Oakland, California. Our books are selected not by a group of editors, but by readers worldwide.

While we've published books by established writers like *Big Fish* author Daniel Wallace and *Star Wars: Rogue One* scribe Gary Whitta, our aim remains surfacing and developing the new author voices of tomorrow.

Previously unknown Inkshares authors have received starred reviews and been featured in *The New York Times*. Their books are on the front tables of Barnes & Noble and hundreds of independents nationwide, and many have been licensed by publishers in other major markets. They are also being adapted by Oscar-winning screenwriters at the biggest studios and networks.

Interested in making your own story a reality? Visit Inkshares. com to start your own project or find other great books.